Moonbeams Too

by

Lyn Miller LaCoursiere

Copyright © 2014 by Lyn Miller
LaCoursiere
All rights reserved.
No part of this book may be
reproduced without
the written permission of the Publisher.
This is a work of fiction.
Names, characters, places and incidents
are used fictitiously. Any resemblance
to actual persons, events
or locales is entirely coincidental.

Cover photo courtesy of Jack Henneman

Cover design by Genny Kieley
& Lyn LaCoursiere

Format
by Genny Kieley

ISBN # 978-1-938990-04-5

Moonbeams Too

An excerpt from Moonbeams Too

Believing Roma Hurst, Daisy O'Dell's best friend and the killer's first victim, has given Daisy valuable information about his ring of deadly assassins; she is forced to flee Birch Lake, in northern Minnesota for Minneapolis, after another "killer for hire" has attempted to take her life. Now safe in the city she is awakened suddenly in the night, as she hears her locked hotel door open quietly. Will she die now?

Hats off to LINDY LEWIS ADVENTURES author, Lyn Miller LaCoursiere for creating another satisfying adventure in the new Moonbeams series. Lindy's younger cousin Daisy O'Dell encounters danger, romance and intrigue around every corner. Lyn's descriptive settings and well developed characters will entertain you as the plot keeps you on the edge of your seat.
Jeff Loven

Lyn is QUEEN of the page turners.
Sue Wilson

Your characters are CHARMING, COLORFUL AND SURPRISING. Enjoy the "ride" as they say. Write on!!!
Judith Granahan

We all live vicariously through LINDY and now DAISY. Adventuresome ladies for sure.
Judy Anderson

Moonbeams Too is a wonderfully written book that will take y

Books by Lyn Miller LaCoursiere

Nightmares and Dreams

Tomorrow's Rain

Sunsets

Suddenly Summer

The Early Years

Silence

Moonbeams

A note from the Author

As a writer, I'm very routine conscious and I've found devoting my early morning to creative thinking is what works best or me. I love the time spent with my characters, and as I place Lindy or Daisy in one of their thrilling episodes, I usually sit back and think, how would I act and react in the same circumstances? I live with and love my people as I write. They lead me on. Like I say, you have to make your own music in life, so writing about my characters' antics is a morning exercise in creativity that makes me smile and keeps me motivated and focused.

My mom, Signe Miller was the first journalist in my family, and with her encouragement I began to write. Although she was an incredibly busy wife with a houseful of ten kids, she was dedicated to writing her column each week for the Thief River Falls, Minnesota *Times* paper. My sisters and I got a taste of writing too, by helping her in gathering the news from around our neighborhood.

I remember that she was so talented in writing reviews of the weddings in the area for the paper. I was always fascinated by her wonderful, vivid and evocative details in describing a bride's gown. And her eloquence in her narration of the attendants dress, the flowers and music.

No one is too young or too old to start writing. We have to visualize our dreams, throw away the roadblocks and take that first step. You don't have to worry about using correct grammar or punctuation, just write, anything. Learn to describe your own feelings, and then give them to a character. And of course embellish!

I think one of the hardest parts of writing for me is marketing my books. First of all, I have to go out and talk to strangers and look professional. When I'm just happy sitting at my computer in an old comfy robe, with my coffee. But I know it's so important for someone of my age to have a focus, so I keep on writing. But a dear sister-in-law has promised that if my stories got too weird in the future, she will let me know.

In the Lindy Lewis Adventures, as well as in Moonbeams and Moonbeams Too, my characters are fictitious, although I do use some characteristics that are similar to some people. I do this with love.

Daisy is younger than her cousin Lindy Lewis, but more mature in her thinking as well as in her life. She has experienced young love, been married and has children. She has a business and is financially secure and has moved from Minneapolis back to her home town of Birch Lake in northern Minnesota to retire in the safety of friends and relatives. And until her good friend Roma Hurst comes back into her life, Daisy is content.

I want to again thank all of you faithful readers who support my writing and hope this book will provide you with many hours of enjoyable reading late into the night. I love you all.

My books are available at Amazon.com in paperback and as e-books. They may also be found at some Minneapolis book stores and libraries, on my web-site or you can contact me personally.

Regards always,
Lyn

Acknowledgements

I wish to thank Jenny and Danielle
in editing this book.
Mary M
again for her technical help.

Also, thanks to my
Nightwriter friends for their
constant vigilance.

This book is dedicated to
Israel Landon
My new great-grandson.

-1-

Daisy O'Dell had left the drapes open in her second floor hotel room in downtown Minneapolis where a sliver of a full moon peeked out from under a cloudy sky. Enough, to vaguely shadow the bedroom, when suddenly she froze as she felt someone's intense stare as they kneeled right next to her and her pillow. She lay defenseless as the stranger watched her. And she knew without a doubt, he was going to kill her, and that he would use his hands!

She struggled to swallow over the fear which stuck in her throat and cut off her scream. The face was so close she could see the pores on the ridge of his nose, and smell his kerosene breath.

Time was at a standstill as this scene stamped itself in her mind. Then her fear suddenly exploded and gave her energy. She spun into action and sat up.

"Oh---," she cried out and clutched the sheet around herself, then realized she was safe in her bed in her hotel room. But an ache hammered away in her head and a few soft moans still escaped from her lips as she huddled under the sheets.

As she lay warmed now in her covers, she whispered, what the hell was that about? She studied her journey through each previous day, to see if this man could have passed, just momentarily, across her path. Her thoughts also went back to the time she had been getting ready for the arrival of her friend Roma, to make her home again in the US. To the worrisome weeks she had spent worrying about what could have happened to her when she didn't show up. Then weeks later, recognizing her after she tossed layers of clothes off that she had taken to wear as a disguise as an overweight person to get away from Gunther Mueller, the man who was a "killer for hire."

Daisy shivered but reminded herself, he was dead now and she had killed him, so he couldn't hurt her anymore. But after the long and tedious reflection, the face in her dream still belonged to a stranger.

Sometime later, she made a call on her cell to Reed Conners back in Birch Lake. When he answered, she asked, "Hello, not too early is it?"

"No, I'm in my office hard at work." She could hear a fax machine humming in the background.

"I thought you were retired." She smiled into the receiver.

"Well, from some things, yeah, but I still like to keep my foot in the door, you know."

"Reed, I'm calling because I've decided to stay here in Minneapolis for a while."

"You are? Can't say I blame you Daisy. But you're not going to pull up stakes from here for good, are you?" he asked.

For a moment Daisy felt torn, after all it was there she planned to stay forever when she had moved back to her home town years ago, and said, "I'm not sure Reed, but I've decided I'm going to take a break before I decide for sure what to do. For all I know, there could be another gun for hire out there waiting for me."

"You need to be very careful and vigilant, Daisy, for anything, or anyone who might look suspicious there and call 911 right away."

"Believe me Reed, I don't intend to take anything lightly."

"Okay. And Daisy, we're watching for anyone looking suspicious hanging around here too, and we're also keeping an eye on your house."

"Good. Thanks. Oh and by the way Reed, I hired one of the neighbors to take care of my lawn. And, I'm having my mail sent to me here." She added as an afterthought.

"Keep in touch Daisy. And let me know if you change addresses."

Determined now to get up and get busy, she remembered that she had another meeting with Billy Miller, the attorney who was taking care of her claim. The claim she had opened after her friend Roma's death, after finding that hand-written will Roma had left, declaring she wanted Daisy to inherit her assets in the event of her death.

Billy Miller's office was on the 39th floor of a building downtown. Reed had been with her that first time, when he had driven her down to Minneapolis and introduced her to Miller.

She stood for a minute to summon all her nerve this morning, then sucked in her breath and stepped into the elevator. She had a phobia about elevators. As a kid, she'd been left in an elevator and the doors had closed and then malfunctioned. She had never forgotten those long scary hours of being locked in that small dark room. Her hand shook as she pushed the button for the 39th floor. Inside she turned to face the wall and put both hands on a railing and got ready. As the enclosure began to move, all she could do was close her eyes and hang on. On the long ride up, she didn't notice the people coming on or getting off until minutes later she felt a tap on her shoulder. Realizing they had stopped, she turned around, and then looked right into the eyes of a stranger. She felt immediate danger! Then saw the stare was from a man, impatient at her obvious slow exodus as he waited to get out.

Daisy gave the stranger back one of her cold stares and took her time moving out of the way. "Bastard," she said under her breath as she steadied herself. Usually taking stairways, she could make it up to a fourth floor, but at times like these she had no choice but to bite the bullet and get into one of those claustrophobic rooms.

"Oh Lord," she whispered as she stepped into her attorney's office and could finally sit down. She took some steadying breaths.

A few minutes later as they sipped coffee in his inner office, he said, "Miss O'Dell, I want to keep you up to date on the progress of your case. I presented the claim to Roma Hurst's family attorneys last week so now we are required to give thirty days for them to counter-claim."

"Okay," Daisy agreed. "But remember, I don't want to get into any kind of court fight about this with her kids."

"You told me that, Miss O'Dell. We'll wait and see what their reaction is."

"I'm sure they will be totally surprised, and then probably hostile. When I saw them at their mother's funeral, of course, they were devastated, so we didn't exchange more than a few conciliatory words to each other.

Billy Miller drummed his fingers on the table. He was a handsome man somewhere in his late fifties.

Graying black hair combed straight back at his temples gave him a sophisticated air. His brown eyes were edged with laugh lines. He was fit and trim and wearing a blue pin-striped suit, a pristine white shirt and a red silk tie.

"Tell me, Miss O'Dell," he went on, "did Miss Hurst ever say anything about any of this to you?"

"No, not a word, I found the note in the bottom of her make-up bag." Daisy ran a hand through her blond hair and blinked back tears. "I guess she figured I would check over her things and find it if anything happened to her."

"Okay, their attorneys will have thirty days to answer, so I'll get back to you promptly, Miss O'Dell." And he shook hands with her and walked with her to the door.

Then she had to get herself down the 39 floors again. This time she angled her way to the back of the elevator and just closed her eyes and held on to a bar. By the time she got down to ground floor, after the stops and starts, her stomach was in an upheaval. After a taxi ride a few blocks back to her hotel, she threw her clothes on a chair and fell into bed. Sick!

And she vowed, she would not go through this again and would request that the attorney meet her, somewhere on the ground.

-2-

Ed Harrison was sometimes called a snob, being brought up by parents that certainly were, but unlike them, he had a delightful sense of humor that made him likable to all his friends, acquaintances and cronies around Birch Lake. Being a well-known bachelor and a rich one too, he was very popular because everyone knew someone who was looking for a prize husband. Him? He just laughed and bought drinks and dated all those unattached and sometimes attached, women around the country. Years ago, he had built his own house and lived in one of the biggest houses in and around Birch Lake. Since his folks had retired to the south, and being the only kid, he had inherited their new and used car business.

Lyn LaCoursiere

Tonight was his fifty-fifth birthday party that he was hosting out on his boat that he had named Mystery, a forty foot formula. It had a lower level with a bedroom, a bathroom and a full service kitchen with a pull out table. He had put the big floating beauty on low and had given his young handyman instructions to stay sober and just circle the lake as he would be busy celebrating. Now he slipped the lock on his bedroom door and continued undressing this lovely new stranger who had come along with someone else to the party. Although, it didn't take long to undo the few ties of a bikini until the stranger stood before him in all her glory.

"Now, let me see what you've got?" she murmured, a slight Scandinavian accent in her sexy voice.

"Without a doubt, it's more than you can take care off," Ed joked and pulled her close.

"Whoa, Eddy it's more than I want." The stranger playfully whispered in his ear.

And after several minutes of bantering back and forth the couple fell on the bed and got down to the serious business of making love, or lust as Ed Harrison thought of it. And after a hasty shower and a splash of cologne he was up top again in minutes.

"Who the hell was that?" Stan, his good friend who owned the Woodsmen Café in town asked after seeing them disappear downstairs.

"Hell, I don't have the foggiest," Ed laughed as he stood at the make-shift bar and poured a generous shot of Gray Goose over ice.

"Any good?" Stan asked.

"You thinking about seconds?" Ed shot back.

"Naw, I got all I can take care of right here," and Stan patted his date on her backside.

Just then another local roared up to the Formula with his boat and tied up to the Mystery, then stepped over the side and with his date joined the dozen people already aboard.

"Hey Reed, good to see you buddy." Ed smiled at his friend. "And Lindy, you're still keeping his bed warm?" He asked good-naturedly.

Lindy laughed. "Keeping it hot is what he says." She smoothed her new white lace cover-up over the tiniest black two-piece she could find in the local store and stepped into her wedgies after carrying them over.

Reed had shed his usual jeans and boots for a Tommy Bahama shirt over beige shorts and flip flops. His tanned trim body looked good even though he was well into his fifties too. He took a small gift wrapped package out of his pocket and thrust it into his host's hand.

"Hey buddy, what's this?" Ed asked.

"Happy birthday my good friend. It's something to keep in your bed on these cool nights coming up soon." Reed commented, then laughed as Ed ripped the paper off his gift and held up a black lace bikini.

"Well, all I'll need then is someone to fit into these." Ed's brown curly hair had fallen down over his forehead as he did a dance step and turn around.

Everyone laughed, tipped their glasses and drank some more.

Someone had put an old CD on the player and suddenly the haunting strains of The Tennessee Waltz began its familiar pattern of memories to this over fifty crowd.

One couple looked into each other's eyes and the years slipped away as they stepped close and Reed Conners and Lindy Lewis swayed together as if over two decades hadn't already sped by.

Ed Harrison stood alone, and was suddenly lonely. He watched his friends and hummed under his breath. Then took out his cell and made a call.

"Hello Daisy," he said, "I'm wondering--.

-3-

Daisy O'Dell sat with Josey, her good friend who had lived in the same cul-de-sac in their old neighborhood in Edina. She was still married to her surgeon, their kids were grown and as she said, she had a full time job entertaining and lunching with their affluent friends. Years ago, when the four kids had finally all gone off to college, and of course, her hubby always busy in the operating room, she had up and sold their home for big bucks and bought a house on Lake Minnetonka. It was a show place; with six bedrooms and six baths, a media room, a kitchen designed right out of a magazine and best of all, a guest house. At first, hubby was pissed at her for not needing his help, but as time went on, he selfishly loved all the niceties it brought.

Josey was a blonde and nearing the big half a century mark, worked out religiously and ran two miles a day. She had a stylist, a masseur, a house cleaner and a personal shopper.

As Daisy had watched her come into Gina's restaurant, she noticed she walked with a slight limp. And she stood up then and gave her a hug, inhaling her expensive Prada cologne.

"I see your limp, how did you get hurt?" She asked her friend.

"Oh, it's nothing, I just lost my footing and slipped." For a minute, Daisy thought she saw hesitation cross Josey's face and asked, "Is it a sprain?"

"No, it's nothing." And to change the subject Josey went on to ask, "What kind of wine should we have today?"

Daisy smiled then and holding up a menu said, "Let's try this new bottle, I see they're advertising."

Josey settled in at their table tucking her purse on a side chair. "I love that, my husband and I had it when we were here a while back."

"I really don't like that much to drink in the afternoon, but we'll take our time and eat a good lunch," Daisy added.

"Well, now girlfriend, tell me what's been going on in your life lately," Josey asked not able to contain her curiosity any longer. "I read about that shooting back in "Timbuktu" or what you call that place you moved to."

"Girlfriend," Daisy remarked dryly, "It's a lovely place right on a lake, but I'm not living there now."

"Whoa, why not?" Josey asked as she rearranged the table things to her liking.

Just then a waiter came over and Daisy ordered the bottle of wine, taking her time to ask questions about the vintner and his location. All the while giving herself time to decide how much she was going to tell her friend.

"Josey," she said now, "do you remember Roma Hurst? She lived just down the block from us in the cul-de-sac."

"Well, of course I do. She was that one from Sweden or somewhere over there." Joscy nodded her head up and down and her blond hair bounced on her shoulders.

"That's her. She was from Norway originally and she married an American and lived here."

"Yes, I remember. But she died? We didn't get the whole story, just what we heard over television and read in the papers. So tell me Daisy, what really happened?"

Josey loved gossip and now her blue eyes sparkled with intensity at the prospect of hearing the real story.

"Roma and I got to be good friends as our boys were both in hockey. We took turns driving those boys at all hours of the day and nights to practice and then we would sit together at games and cheer them on." Daisy took a breath and reached for the glass of water the waiter had just placed on their table, then went on, "Neither of our husbands had time to support the kids in their sports so we spent a lot of time together."

"I sure am familiar with that, my kids never knew their father then either," Josey murmured.

"No excusing them, but to their way of reasoning they were busy making way in their prosperous careers and it was our jobs to raise the kids," Daisy said looking around the beautiful dining room with its white linen covered tables, and huge colorful paintings hung on the walls. "Damn," she said then, "I sure could go for a cigarette."

"I gave up that habit years ago, but I loved it. My doc said, 'Leave it or you will die,'" Josey remarked.

Daisy ran a hand through her silvery blond hair and blinked her brown eyes. "I know."

"Go on and tell me the rest of the story," Josey exclaimed bending in close.

"Well, you read then that Roma was shot by her boyfriend who also was from over there."

"Yes, I remember that. Was she cheating or something?"

"No, nothing like that. You see, she didn't know that he was a killer for hire and when she found out she tried to get away from him!"

"Oh for God's sake!" Josey exclaimed and put her hand over her mouth. "You mean a real killer, a real one?" Her blue eyes were large.

"He was real alright." Then Daisy figured what the hell, she might as well tell her the rest. "You see, she never thought he would follow her here to the U.S. But he did and he killed her. So then I shot the fucker!"

"I didn't know that," Josey said then as her hands gripped the table's edge.

"For my protection, that was kept quiet." Daisy busied herself then sipping the wine the waiter had set down and poured for them.

"Good God, you shot the killer?" Josey asked just to make sure.

"I did. You see he came looking for me too, after he had killed her, thinking she had told me all about him. Well, she had told me some, and I had to hide out. But in the end he found me."

Josey had been drinking her wine like it was Kool-Aid. "Wow," was all she could utter from time to time.

"You won't believe this, but he put poisonous snakes in her luggage and when she got to my house and opened her suitcases up they got loose." Daisy shook her head slowly at this. "My lovely home," she mused and looked off in the distance. "Well, I had it fumigated or whatever they do."

"Good Lord," was all Josey could still exclaim.

"It's been a busy summer," Daisy said and put a smile on her face. "And, I might stay here in the city and find a house."

"Really? How exciting," Josey exclaimed. "We've got a lot of catching up to do, my friend. Oh Lord, I can't get over you having to shoot someone!"

Daisy ran a hand through her hair ruffling it this time, then smoothed it down. "I was lucky, I was just a few seconds ahead of him or he would have killed me. Josey, I've had many nightmares about this, and still do, but my doctor says they'll subside gradually."

"Oh my God, do you want to come and stay with me for a while until you get over them?" Josey asked.

Daisy wanted to say yes, but didn't dare mention, if someone was still out there looking for her, she didn't want to stay with another friend and bring her into the equation. She might be killed as well. But of course, she didn't want to bring it up now and scare her to death and instead said, "Thanks Josey, that's lovely of you but I have reservations at the hotel for thirty days."

"Well, for God's sake break it," Josey insisted.

"No Josey, I'll tell you more later. Now, let's order something fabulous to eat that goes with this wine." Daisy smiled at her friend and brushed at the crumbs on her lap from the bread they were dipping in olive oil and parmesan.

"Well, at least tell me, have you met someone rich and dashing in that town of yours?"

"Hmm-, well maybe," was all Daisy was prepared to tell. "But now tell me, really, how did you hurt your ankle?"

Josey realized she had no one else to confide in so she said to her friend, "well, here's my news, I'm leaving my husband. He's become abusive, and that's why I have a bad ankle, I was trying to get away from him."

And the two women sat together for several hours and talked, chipping away at the years gone by.

Lyn LaCoursiere

-4-

Ed Harrison lifted his head off the pillow and looked at the stranger who was asleep on the one next to his. He groaned inwardly and wondered who the hell this woman was. As he lay there in bed, he felt the room move then realized he was still downstairs on his boat, out on Birch Lake and the chop was from another boat out there on the water. Or at least that's where he was the last he remembered.

Oh man, as he swallowed he found he had a hell of a sore throat and now it all started to come back. He'd been cheering the party on as some female was stripping to the tune of the old song called "Fever". He'd been right there catching her clothes as she tossed them in the air. Of course, there wasn't too many to begin with.

How much time did it take to untie a few strings of a bikini? Maybe half a dozen couples stood around watching, mostly drunk and stoned and after that, Ed drew a blank.

When did the party stop and where did everybody go? He should try to stand and go up top and see if they were all still up there passed out. Or what? Would he find some bodies floating in the water? Oh Christ, he mumbled and tossed the covers back. He looked at the woman on the pillow again, and then the memory came back to him of her sitting on him rocking the boat. Oh hell, he swore, who the fuck did she say she was again?

He didn't dare try standing up fast or he just might pass out, so he took it slow. His hair hung in his face and he swiped at it now impatiently as he first sat up, then raised himself slowly from the bed and was on his feet. Looking down at himself, he realized he was stark naked. For Christ sake, had he joined the woman in the strip?

He slowly bent over and found his beige shorts on a chair. It was tricky getting them on without falling over but he got it done and finally trudged up the stairway topside.

Shit, was all he could say when he saw the scene. No one was there, except two gulls eating crumbs from the table and crapping everywhere.

"God damn it, get outta here, dumb fucks!" He waved his arms and yelled. Then started the motor and checked that out. Observing his own rule, always before he allowed himself to walk off his boat, he needed to clean the mess. Swearing again as he found a garbage bag he bent over to pick up glasses and left over chips, napkins and beer caps. Even the little black lace bikini underwear, Reed had given him for a birthday present lay on the floor covered in refuse.

Ed picked it up and shook it out and wondered how Daisy would look in it, then suddenly remembered his call to her. What would she have thought if she had seen him later?

With that he cussed himself for being such a pig. Goddamnit, he wasn't really such a bad guy, was he? Normally, he led a pretty clean life, or so he thought. But if you asked some of the locals maybe their stories would be different. But that would be from some of the church ladies. He had to laugh when he thought of some of the tight assed ones he saw around town. Well, God bless them. They had a hard enough job keeping their men on the straight and narrow in Birch Lake where nothing exciting ever happened to them.

And he had a reputation to uphold as he liked to think. What would the townspeople talk about if not about him?

At least his thoughts kept him busy as he cleaned and polished his prize back to normal. Goddamn, it would be a long time again before he would let it get so bad. And just then he jumped when a voice behind him whispered, "Eddie, come back down and let's do it again?"

Ed wiped the sweat off his face and turned to look at the woman. He frowned when he still could not remember her name. "Ahh-," he mumbled not at all in the mood, "I'd love to doll, but I've got to get this done and park it."

"Really? I'm so disappointed." Now he saw she was small in size, but then noticed her bulging muscles.

Remembering her accent and taking a second look at her he asked, "Where did you say you're from?"

She smiled, "I didn't. But I'm not from around here."

Ed had been down on his knees cleaning the floor and put the scrub brush down in the bucket of water. "Well, I gathered that," he said rising up. "Are you visiting someone around here then?"

"Yes, like that." As she came topside he saw now she had used one of his shirts and tied it up on her midriff over her bikini bottom. "I hope you don't mind that I borrowed your shirt, I'll get it back to you."

Seeing it was one of his Tommy Bahamas, he couldn't keep the pissed look off his face and said, "Your cover-up is on the chair right over there."

"Are you soon done cleaning?" She asked and picked it up, not asking if she could help.

"Soon," he remarked. "I need to go into town to take care of some business, so I can drop you at where you're staying."

"Oh, I don't want us to be over so soon! Will you wait there while I shower and change and we can spend the day together?" Her long brown hair hung limply around her face which was devoid of make-up. And now in the sunlight Ed could see she was much older then she had looked last night, and with those muscles, looked almost manly.

Embarrassed that he didn't know her name and too late now to ask he said, "Give me another fifteen minutes while I finish up and then we can go."

"Okay," she turned and disappeared down below and he wondered again, who the hell is she? And for some intuitive reason he did not want to bring her back to his house, so decided to tie up in town next to the Woodsmen Cafe where they could have breakfast, and he'd see then how to play this.

A few minutes later, the Formula was shining clean and Ed started the motor and they roared back to Birch. Coming into the café the usual line-up of locals took up space at the counter and they were met with a chorus of various greetings, which Ed returned as they followed Flo to a booth.

After being seated and already a pot of coffee in front of them, Ed asked again curiously hoping to pry some information out of her, "I'm sorry I don't remember who you said you were visiting here in Birch." He noticed she was still looking at his friends at the counter, in fact studying them.

"I'm staying with some friends here."

"Who?" Ed asked. "I know everybody around here."

"No, you wouldn't know them I'm sure, they're new." Now the woman took up the menu and raised her hand and motioned for Flo to come back. And after detailed directions, she ordered her breakfast.

Reed Conners came over then and slid into the booth beside Ed. "Good morning," he said, "I see you're both alive and well."

"Alive, but not well." Ed remarked dryly.

Reed looked pointedly at the women. "I didn't get your name last night, who are you?" He laughed to soften the issue.

The woman laughed too. "I didn't know I was a woman of interest. My name is Ursula and I'm from Wisconsin."

After that they talked and visited, but when they got up to leave, as was his nature to know exactly to whom he was letting get close, Reed slipped her empty water glass in his pocket and later that day dropped it off with the BOCA office in Bemidji.

Ed dropped Ursula off then with her friends who lived in that new house on the edge of town who owned the local funeral home.

A small shiver cursed over his body as he walked her to the door and she raised her lips to his in a kiss and said, "I'll be seeing you again soon, Eddie."

But something made him think, no thanks.

As his head cleared that day, Ed remembered his call to Daisy and their plan to get together the next week-end in Minneapolis to see some shows and celebrate his birthday. She had said she'd reserve a room for him at her hotel and that was okay with him. During the time she had stayed with him when the crazed German had been after her, he had felt a stirring protection come over him, a feeling that was new to him. Sure, he'd had some relationships that might have led somewhere over time, but now after so many years, he'd thought he was destined to always be just a "good-time Charley".

But there was something about Daisy that made him stop and pucker his forehead in thought.

Ed Harrison was in his early fifties and all that day he drank water in an effort to get the alcohol flushed out of his body, then spent hours in his gym. By evening he had himself back in control and after a second shower that day, combed his black curly hair back off his face and trimmed his mustache. At six two, he was a handsome man, still slim around the waist and in good health, but he wouldn't stay that way for long if he imbibed too often like he had that last night.

He got in his shiny Cadillac Escalade then and drove down town to Harrison Motors, his new and used car business. The lot looked busy and he hurried into the showroom and then to his office. And for the rest of the day he was busy with potential customers, who wanted to do business with the owner. Then to his consternation who should amble in at the close of the day but Ursula, the woman from his bed the night before.

"Hello, Eddie," she laughed, "I found you!"

Ed tried to hide his angst. Feeling he was being stalked, he wondered how he could get away from her again, he asked, "Ursula, are you looking to buy a car?"

"I might," she answered.

"What would you be interested in?"

"Oh, I only drive a Mercedes." Ursula had put her long hair up in a pony-tail, which seemed tight enough to make her squint. She was wearing white shorts, a red tube top, and was braless he could see, and stood braced in high heels. From a distance, she looked like a knock out, but up close and personal, Ed knew the real Ursula, and had no intention of getting hooked up with her again.

Although he didn't want to blow a possible sale, he smiled politely. "Well, tell me what you have in mind and if I don't have it here I can have it in a few hours."

"I don't doubt you can. But, I'll have to let you know later. Hey, how about taking me to dinner at the casino tonight, but for now Eddie, I'm wondering if you have a manicurist in your town."

He froze. Daisy was a manicurist. Then Ed covered his consternation and shook his shoulders and said, "No, sorry Ursula I don't know any."

Ursula smiled thinly, "Oh, you don't. I thought you would."

For Ed to acknowledge it further either way, he would be giving away a sudden dreaded thought.

"Sorry," he said then and fortunately his cell phone rang. "Important long distance," he mumbled and turned and went back to his office and closed the door.

"Goddamn," Reed said to him on his cell, "I think this woman is another killer looking for Daisy!"

Lyn LaCoursiere

-5-

She could tell the man was lying through his teeth. After all, it was not possible to live in this gimp of a burg and not know all its residents and what they did to make a living. She had seen the lie flicker quickly in Ed's eyes when she'd asked if he knew where she could find a manicurist, and he'd emphatically said no, he didn't. She hadn't found a single trace of the woman, only that her house was closed up tight.

Amelia Arickson, or Ursula as she was known in the U.S. put the dark cigarette with its long black holder down in the ashtray as she sat in the bathtub in her benefactor's home. It was comfortable enough with all the latest conveniences here in this freaking funeral home but nothing like her spacious loft in the hamlet in

Oslo. There, she had a spa fit for a king, which she had paid big money to install a few years ago, when she had fallen into this million dollar business. Cripes, she could hardly believe her good fortune when she had found this ad in the local paper for a 'unique person to conduct some occasional business for an extraordinary party. Must be free to travel to anywhere in the world.'

It had taken numerous interviews with this man, Mr. Jonas, to even be considered. A romance with him, and a then a shooting where she killed a woman in what she thought was self-defense but soon realized it was a double cross. She had no choice or she would be turned in to the law for murder and possibly go to prison for life.

Whomever Mr. Jonas worked for held it over her head unless she hired on. But she knew she'd have to go to the ends of the earth to get away from them is she ever wanted to change her job description. For now, her order was to find Daisy O'Dell and eliminate her, which sounded easy enough with a big payoff.

Amelia was born in an orphanage in Norway and grew up being handed from one foster family to another. It wasn't because she was an incorrigible youngster, but because the homes were poor and couldn't always keep an extra child any longer to feed and clothe, and so she grew up being needy; both for friends and resources and made a living cleaning houses and doing laundry for the rich.

Her only mediator for this job had been Mr. Jonas in Oslo, who had interviewed her numerous times, lead her on to believe he loved her, then set her up in that shooting, and double crossed her. And sure, he had kept her from going to prison with his alibi for her, but she still hurt from his betrayal, but "God dam," she was not going to think about that anymore. Someday, she would get even with the piker.

As she sat in the bathtub, her thoughts went to the man she had just spent the night with. Ed was his name and she'd met him at the local and he'd invited her to a party out on his boat that evening on the lake. His water was nothing more than a puddle as she was used to the wide open spaces of the Atlantic. He was okay for a one-nighter, but not much of a lover and if they spent more time together she would have to teach him to go slow and learn to enjoy the finer arts of love-making. But for now, she'd gotten a good look at his friends so she'd stick around town for a while to pick up on any info she could about Daisy O'Dell's whereabouts.

-1- 7

A week had gone by and today Daisy left Billy Miller's office after hearing the claim for Roma's estate was going along without any snags. When she thought about it though, she felt guilty claiming those assets which should go to Roma's sons. But then, according to Miller, Roma's family was well taken care off. But then too, maybe she should call the boys and see for herself. Her thoughts were heavy as she maneuvered the Porsche through the late afternoon traffic in Minneapolis. She was hungry and decided to stop at Gina's for a light dinner and then go back to her hotel for a good night's rest.

Coming up to the restaurant, the two guys who had worked there for several decades greeted her. She'd heard they were street bums when they were young and Gina had taken them in and promised them a job if they cleaned up their act and they had stayed clean ever since. Now, they two were a part of Gina's devoted family.

"Hello, Daisy," they said in unison as they opened the car door and waited for her to step out. "Nice to see you, Gina will be happy to set eyes on you again." One whisked her car away, while the other held the door open for her into the restaurant as Daisy pressed a bill into his hand.

Daisy always loved coming to this place. In the early years when she had been newly married, she'd pinch pennies for a special night out. When she had a few dollars saved, she and her husband would go downtown to that first place Gina owned and treat themselves to prime steaks and a movie. So many years ago, went through her thoughts as she stepped into the foyer and waited with a group of patrons.

Busy with her reservations, Gina never changed, she saw. This afternoon, her blonde hair shone in the light done up in a French twist with wisps curling over her cheeks. Her make-up was elegantly done and her dress was a black a-line. And of course, her feet were enclosed in three inch black sling-backs.

"Daisy," Gina exclaimed then and pulled her into a hug, "I didn't know you were in town."

Daisy smiled at her old friend. "I've just been here a few days now, but I plan on staying around for a while."

"Really, that's marvelous." Gina exclaimed stepping back and looking her over. "I've got to say my dear you're looking good for what I heard you went through."

"I guess Birch made the papers all over the country." Daisy shook her head as she talked.

"Well, I keep in touch with Reed, you know." Gina put her helper in charge and took Daisy's arm and they walked into the bar. "I need a break, so let's have a cocktail, while you decide what we can fix for you to eat, shall we?"

"Paul, look who came back to civilization," she joked to the bartender as they hopped up on stools. And he came around the bar to give Daisy a hug too.

"Good to see you." Daisy smiled at him. "And Paul, I'll have a Stoli's Martini please."

"A woman who knows a good one!" He laughed.

Gina looked at her now after they settled. "Tell me, what you meant when you said you were staying here."

Daisy tucked the hemline of her lime green dress in around her knees as she perched on the bar stool, then hung her oversize patent leather purse on the arm rest. Her platinum earrings and bracelets sparkled in the low lights as she ran a hand through her short spiked silvery hair.

"I may not want to stay in Birch Lake any longer. So I might put my house up for sale."

"Really? It's so beautiful," Gina replied.

"It still is, but not for me." Daisy said. "But I'll tell you more about it later. Now I just want to enjoy the company of you two."

Gina smiled. "Sweetie, that's good enough for us. But tell me first what kind of house you might look for here?"

"You know, I'm thinking of a downtown loft. I've got an appointment to look at what's going on over at the old Grain Belt Brewery building."

"I hear that some of the condos that are ready and for sale are priced at several million." Gina said as she watched Paul mix the martini and place it on the bar for Daisy, then reach to the top shelf for her special bottle.

"I'm thinking of changing things up. Maybe I'll live here in the summer and find something down south by the ocean to winter at."

"Now that's a good idea, Daisy. Enjoy the best of both worlds, I always say."

"How about you Gina, have you taken time off and traveled?" Daisy asked her friend.

"No, not lately, although I have someone I may go to Paris with this coming spring."

"Really, this a special beau?" Daisy asked.

"Well, heavens at my age, they're all special beaus!" And the two beautiful women laughed together and enjoyed their own company. Although Gina was at least a decade older than Daisy, no one would ever ask her age or for that matter, would she ever divulge it to anyone. But her magnetism was just one of the traits she held that made her a perfect fit to have run a successful business all these years. She took a delicate sip of her hundred year old bourbon and smiled at her friend.

"Did you go to Ed Harrison's party on his boat last weekend up there in Birch?" she asked Daisy now.

"No," Daisy answered. "I was down here by then. I was sorry I missed it though."

"Well, hearing about their parties, I think I would count myself lucky to be away when one is held." Gina shook her head.

"Ed Harrison helped me a lot that last week I was there, and we got to be pretty good friends."

"Well, yes he's a good guy. But, maybe he has too much money and time on his hands." Gina turned on her stool to check on her helper as she talked.

"What do you know about him, Gina?" Daisy asked curiously.

"I knew his folks well. A whole group of us hung around together back then. Of course they were somewhat older than me."

"Really," Daisy listened.

"I've known Reed Conners since his college days. And before he died, Tanner Burke too. You see, they both worked for me in those days as cooks when I first started my business. Eddie Harrison was in the group, but he didn't need to work as he came from money."

"Small world," Daisy murmured.

"Daisy, didn't you come from up there in the boonies too?" Gina asked then.

"Yes, but I didn't get around much then." Daisy took a swallow of her martini and savored the smooth vodka as it slid down her throat. She tried to still the thoughts, that always came tumbling back to haunt her when she was reminded of her very young days growing up in the north.

-6-

Ed Harrison slept ten hours after drinking gallons of water and then sat in his spa to sweat the alcohol out of his system. Jesus, he didn't think he'd have drunk that much if he hadn't been so pissed at hearing Daisy's plans.

He had just started thinking it was time he should finally settle down. This might be the right woman for him, after spending so much time together those last days when that crazed killer had been loose around town. He'd dreamt about it a few times, even seen her herding a bunch of their kids to school in one of his sturdy vehicles. He glimpsed her image and imagined she'd gained a few pounds around the hips after having that number of kids she had blessed him with.

Lyn LaCoursiere

Now as he sat and felt the sweat drip off his body in the sauna, he cussed at his naivety. He should have known better than to expect a woman like her to be satisfied with a small town bum like him. After all, she was beautiful and independent and had been on her own for years.

He tossed another dipper of water on the hot rocks and listened to it sizzle as he thought about Daisy O'Dell. He remembered her slightly from their young days at the local high school. He'd been an A-plus student and a snob back then. He only ran with a couple of other rich kids who drove new cars and their only feat-acomplli was to see who could get the most girls to give up their virginity. He remembered they'd all tried to get Daisy Bird, as she was known then, to go for rides with them but she'd always turned up her nose, walked away and shook her head. Even though they pretended not to care he'd had to give her kudos' for resisting their taunts.

He remembered hearing that she had moved down to Minneapolis to attend college at the U of M, then later married and settled there. He'd seen her a few times over those several decades when she'd come back to Birch Lake to attend reunions. He'd met her husband then who seemed like a regular guy and also her kids. He'd seen she'd developed into a real looker, as a slim, good looking woman who wore her brown hair now in a platinum blonde short do.

Maybe he should have tried to come on to her these weeks to let her know he was interested, but he could never find the right time since the whole town had been on alert against that mad man. He'd had high hopes lately about getting together to declare his feelings until he'd talked to her.

Their conversation had included the usual greetings but had taken a sudden turn for the worse when she said that she was thinking of selling her home here in Birch and going to look for something to buy down there in Minneapolis.

"You mean you're not coming back to Birch Lake to live?" He'd asked.

When she'd tried to explain that she couldn't ever relax enough to live in her house since those snakes had been in there. She said that no matter how many times she'd have to have it fumigated, she still would constantly be looking in the corners for more.

"Well, just sell it then and rebuild," he'd suggested easily. "Something bigger and better if you like."

"No-," she'd answered. "I think I will stay here and look around for something else."

"Well hell, I thought you were happy living here," he'd exclaimed.

"I was, until I lost my best friend there and then that Athena weirdo died in my kitchen."

Then he couldn't hold his feelings in any longer and said, "I was thinking maybe we had a chance to build a relationship together."

Lyn LaCoursiere

She hadn't said anything for a while, then replied, "Oh Ed, how nice, I'm not looking for a relationship right now. But we can still see each other as friends."

But he'd felt the letdown and tried to cover it by a joking remark, then he'd quickly ended their conversation.

Now a few weeks later, he was still upset and today he still felt sad. Although he was a handsome man, lived in a beautiful home on the lake, had a thriving business and money to burn, he was very lonely.

As he toweled off after a shower he stood in front of a full length mirror and took a good look at himself. Over the years, he'd been told he resembled Robert Wagner, that old movie actor. But he couldn't see it and leaning in closer, he saw those lines in his face had deepened and his hair had gotten grayer around the sides. Maybe if he sucked in his belly so his stomach looked flat it would help, but who could go around all day holding his breath to do that?

"Jesus", he muttered as he dressed for work again. I hope that woman doesn't show up today. When she had stopped in the day before, he had come out of his office after taking a phone call, he'd been glad she'd probably taken the hint and taken off. Good riddance, he didn't have time for any more dalliance.

The late summer day was a kaleidoscope of colors and smells as he drove the few blocks through his neighborhood. The air was moist with early morning dew which somewhat held just a touch of mildew from all the recent rain, and the vibrant colors of marigolds, gardenias and holly hocks in the gardens soothed his frayed nerves. Coming in to his car lot, he saw the rows of late model cars and especially the luxury Cadillac's and Lincolns sparkled in the sunlight. His crew always knew how to run the show if he was not there, but then he was always good to them too.

He parked the Cadillac Escalade in the back and went directly to his office, but not seeing his foreman in the showroom was unusual because he always kept a close eye on the merchandise. Then he didn't remember seeing his salesman outside in the lot either, or his mechanic in the shop.

Where the hell were they? He muttered. And as he opened the door into his office, the first thing he saw was the barrel of a semi-automatic assault rifle pointing directly at him. He stood frozen stock still in the doorway.

"Been waiting for you lover," the woman without a name whispered as she sat in his chair at his desk.

"What the hell--," Ed yelled. "Where are my men?"

"Who?" She smiled smugly.

"What did you do? Who the hell are you?" Ed managed to ask but a sick feeling crept into his thoughts. "Where are my men?" he yelled again in sudden fear and began to charge at her. As he got close she jammed the barrel into his chest.

"Hold it lover. Oh, I will shoot you, but not just yet."

Ed took a step back. "Answer me, who are you?"

"Well, we got to know each other pretty well at your party, although, you haven't been treating me very nice since then. Incidentally lover, don't you remember, my name is Ursula."

"Okay, what do you want?" Ed yelled again but he already knew as a wave of terror tore at his gut.

The woman pulled her billed cap down lower over her face which was devoid of any make-up and not even a strand of her hair stuck out around it. The collar from her blue denim shirt stood up.

She got to her feet. "Okay lover, before I shoot you, I want to know where to find your girlfriend, Daisy O'Dell?"

"Yeah? Well, I want to know where my men are?"

Just about then, Ed heard banging and yelling coming from the next room which was a lunchroom. "Hey guys, are you all alright in there?" Ed yelled.

"Yeah, but the bitch tied us up!" resonated through the walls.

"Are you all alright?" Ed yelled again just to make sure.

"Yeah, yeah."

"So you see Eddie, I didn't shoot them yet. Now where is that bitch O'Dell?"

Ed swallowed hard. He'd hung up feeling sorry for himself after Daisy had declared her intentions, and hadn't asked where she was staying.

His heart began to thud when he said he didn't know, and he felt the gun barrel dig deeper into his chest as he stood defenseless in front of the killer for hire.

Lyn LaCoursiere

-7-

Daisy O'Dell sat with her friend Gina at Gina's restaurant in downtown Minneapolis and leisurely sipped her Stoli's martini. But when she was asked about being from Birch Lake in northern Minnesota, she hesitated and her face took on a stony look. She sat silently, seemingly intent on savoring the smooth flow of the liquor as it slid down her throat. But her thoughts were going a mile a minute as she fought to control them.

Would she ever get over that guilty feeling of letting her siblings down, when she had packed her suitcases and left the family store in Birch Lake, leaving her brothers to slave away for their father. Although the family owned a business, they were poor, and God, she couldn't have spent another day in that place they called "The Feed Store."

Her two brothers were ages sixteen and ten years old at that time. Their two story house that stood on the wrong side of town had a kitchen and a living room downstairs and two bedrooms upstairs. No doors for privacy and no bathroom until her eighth grade. Daisy had slept in the same room as her brothers, but she had a cot off in a corner. When she got to be eleven years old, she strung a wire around her corner and hung old sheets for walls when she found the boys were sneaking peeks at her when she undressed. Bath time consisted of using a small basin in that fort-like room, with a special cake of soap that her mother had given her for her birthday. It was called Cashmere Bouquet.

Over the years, Daisy's mother had been handy using a sewing machine and when she started her freshman year in high school, she had two new outfits to wear.

This school was larger with a lot more students who came from further away. She had always been aware of being poor, but so many were in her small world. But now, she was painfully aware, as she met young girls from prominent families in town, who dressed in brand new store bought outfits.

Daisy's studies had come easy for her. And when she graduated from high school with an A plus average, she was invited to attend the U of M tuition free. When she interviewed with one of the schools principals and mentioned she couldn't accept because she didn't have anywhere to live, the principal found a family with an extra room and extra love to extend to some worthy scholar. So Daisy moved in and was finally able to enjoy her own private room with a bathroom all her own. The years sped by for her then as she excelled in her studies for interior design; a career she had dreamed about all her life. Then she struck out on her own and interviewed for a well-established company in Minneapolis where she was hired. Only to enjoy several years and then she met and married a young doctor, got pregnant and began her job as a stay at home mom.

She was still lost in her reverie, but was brought back to the present when Gina asked, "Did you know Reed Conners then?"

Daisy shook her head. "Not then, he was a few years older and only came to Birch for the summers, as his folks owned a cabin by the lake." Daisy answered.

"That's right, he grew up in Williston way up there in the boonies as I recall." Gina laughed.

Daisy nodded. "That's much further north."

"Reed worked for me for a few years back then while he was here studying for his law degree at the U of M." Gina added. "That was when my place was known as the 'Greasy Spoon' to the college kids."

"Long time ago," Daisy murmured.

"So, my dear," Gina turned to her, "you're thinking of relocating to our fair city again? Now, if you need help with anything, please don't hesitate to call me Daisy."

"Thank you, I'll remember that." And Daisy planned to, and after another hour or so, she slipped off her stool and thanked Gina and friends for making her fell welcome.

The rest of the day was free of any commitments and Daisy felt a tremendous relief at not having to see the attorney or be anywhere on cue. She walked down the main street of downtown Minneapolis and reacquainted herself with the familiar shops along the way. One of her old haunts had been the City Library at the Y at the end of Main. Taking a breath to go up the familiar high entrance steps, she saw now, decades later, it had been renovated and extended to twice its original size with numerous new rooms for its tombs of old greats and digital machines. Once inside, and finding the area of new releases, Daisy filled her arms with hard-covers and found a cozy corner and sat. She was soon engrossed in a new book by one of her favorite authors.

She had put her cell phone on vibrate, and left it in her purse, but now several hours later as she collected her things, she casually noticed that it was vibrating.

She saw that she had calls from both Jesse and Reed Conners, and even from someone from the Minneapolis Police Department by the name of John Murphy.

What in the world--, she murmured as she connected to Reed's number first.

"Daisy, you need to get out of that hotel right away. In about thirty minutes Ursela, the killer will be there!"

"Reed for Christ's sake, you mean here?" She struggled to say, then faltered at going on.

"Yes Daisy, listen there's no time, just get miles away from that hotel now. Call me and let me know where you are."

Lyn LaCoursiere

-8-

Ed Harrison stood stock still as the woman jammed the .22 into his chest.

"One more time cowboy, where is Daisy O'Dell?" she whispered. "And I hope you realize I'm very serious."

"Listen bitch," Ed didn't care if he pissed her off, "whoever you are, I told you I don't know!" But he did know immediately who she was.

The woman, who said her name was Ursula, calmly turned toward the wall of his office and fired into it. A low scream emanated from the other side, as the next room was where the other guys were tied up.

"You fucking bitch, you've hurt one of my men!" Ed yelled at her. For Christ's sake, how could he have been in bed with her? She was the devil! She stood defiantly before him in her denims, no make-up and boots and didn't resemble the painted bikini clad sex pot she'd looked like that night on his boat. Of course, he was pretty wasted by that time.

"You better take me seriously cowboy," she growled now. "Or, next time I will send two shots in there."

Ed did not like to be told what to do, not even by this gun slinging bitch, but these were his men, and his townspeople. His only hope was to keep her talking and hope someone was close by and heard what was going on and would call for help and get Jesse. Unless, he could get hold of the .22 she held pointed right at his heart. But, as if she read his mind, she took a few steps back.

"I'm waiting, and I'll ask again, nicely even. Tell me where to find your girlfriend." He did notice she had a faint accent. He wasn't very good at dialects, but it sounded Scandinavian or even German.

"Oh, I take you very seriously. Now Ursula," he said swallowing over his hatred, "listen to me. I can't tell you where she is because I didn't ask."

"Really! Don't take me for a fool." Her face took on a stony reddish glare.

"Believe me, I was pissed when I talked to her last night and hung up." Ed said really nervous now. For Christ's sake, was he going to let this skinny washed out looking hag get the best of him? Normally no, not for a minute if it just involved him. But, here he was responsible for his men who were all family guys with wives and kids. He had to do something to save them from more harm from this crazy woman. But he almost lost it when she suddenly fired another shot, this time it was inches over his head. He had literally felt the shift in the air as it passed over.

"Hold it, hold it," he yelled then, "Stop, I'll tell you what I know!"

"Yeah? How come I don't trust you, but here, put these on first." She reached in a pocket and brought out a pair of handcuffs and tossed them at him. "Now hook up to that refrigerator door and then talk."

Ed did as she said, and now stood shackled to the refrigerator.

"Okay, cowboy spill it!" She stood with her boots braced on her heels with the .22 pointed squarely at him.

Ed cleared his throat. "Honest to God, here's all I know, I didn't ask where Daisy was staying , because I was pissed at her for leaving, the only thing I know for sure is when she was in Minneapolis before, she stayed at this hotel called "The Grand.""

"You expect me to believe that?" She whispered, and only taking the .22 off him for a second, she swung around and fired two more shots, this time back into the next room. This time he heard another of his men let out a low horrible scream.

"Oh Christ, stop it!" Ed yelled back at her. She was lightning good. There hadn't been enough time for him to knock that .22 out of her hands earlier, but then she had to be good, to be a "gun for hire" he had to figure. "Bitch, you'll have to shoot me too because that's all I know."

"Well, then that's what I'll do!" And with both hands on the gun again she took expert aim at his legs and fired, then abruptly turned and fled out the door and in seconds she was gone.

Jesse just missed getting there by several seconds as a customer arriving on the car lot had heard the shots and called for help. He found Ed Harrison still handcuffed to the refrigerator door, but slumped in a bloody heap. But Ed managed to mumble, "The guys next door, she shot my men."

Jesse cut the handcuffs with his wire cutter that hung on his belt and Ed sagged to the floor and went silent.

"Come on Ed, I got help on the way, but wake up!"

Ed opened his eyes wide and grabbed Jesses' shirt front. "I had to tell her Daisy is at the Grand Hotel in Minneapolis. We have to tell her to get out of there!" Then Ed Harrison was silent as he lost consciousness.

-9-

After Jesse had cut Ed loose from being handcuffed to the refrigerator, Ed slid to the floor and lay in his own blood.

"I'm getting help buddy, hang on," Jesse whispered as soon as he got his voice, and taking Ed's jacket from the back of a chair tucked it around him. Then Jesse ran into the lunchroom at Harrison Motors. The walls and floor were covered with blood where two of the men lay bleeding. The third lay duck taped to a chair lying on its side on the floor.

"God almighty," Jesse groaned as he called for the ambulance, and since they only had one in town, he called the fire department and yelled for more help. He also called for Doc to come down and bring his wagon in case. Then went over and looked at the men. One had a head wound and the other one looked dead. The third man in the chair didn't have any visible wounds that Jesse could see, but was unresponsive.

For the next hour, the place buzzed with activity as the wounded were transported to Bemidji, the nearest hospital. And, the one unfortunate enough to have been killed, they covered gently and was left to lay as there wasn't anything to be done for him. Wally had been a salesman; a good friend of Ed's, and had a wife and four teen-agers.

Jesse closed up the business end of Harrison Motors and waited for the BOCA to get there again. It was evening by the time they had all they needed for one day and he could lock the doors. He called the hospital and found out Ed had been shot in both knees but had made it through surgery and was sleeping, while the other two men were holding their own.

Reed Conners had come over minutes after hearing the news that morning from a neighbor and thank God, he had been there to help over-stressed Jesse all day. Jesse also sent his two deputies to the hospital in Bemidji to guard the injured. "And I repeat, do not leave their sides unless you have a security guard take your post. Be ready to shoot to kill! As the killer could come in any disguise and try to finish them off."

Later that night, as Reed and Jesse sat in the Woodsman Café, Reed commented, "Well by now, Daisy should have gotten to a new location." Neither one had eaten much all day except for some doughnuts someone had left for them.

"Good, good. So, we know now that this was done by this woman who came out of nowhere to Ed's boat party." Jesse's hand shook as he lifted his cup of coffee to his lips.

"Well, she's got to be someone from across the pond again, sent to kill Daisy. You better send her prints and her physical description to Mac at the FBI, and let him know that she has killed and wounded people here today."

"Yup, you're right," Jesse agreed. "Oh yeah, did you have a chance to talk to Murphy down there in the cities again?" He asked then.

"Not since this morning, I've got a call in for him so it should be anytime." Reed had brought John Murphy up to speed on the latest when he'd contacted him earlier, after warning Daisy to get away from the hotel she was staying in. "I gave him the description of this woman then too."

Flo came over then with a loaded tray with the evening's special of roast beef with mashed potatoes and gravy, creamed fresh vegetables and hot popovers.

"Okay boys, I want to see clean plates when you're done." She smiled at them and whisked away on her new crepe sole shoes. The guys were silent as they enjoyed every last crumb.

Later, Reed's cell rang as they were drinking their coffee and Ed Harrison's voice echoed in his ear.

"Reed," he whispered gruffly, "How are my guys?"

"Ed, glad to hear you're awake now, tell me, how you are?" Reed asked hurriedly not wanting to tell him about Wally's death yet.

"I'm hooked up to all kinds of fucking things, and I hurt like hell. But I'll make it. How are my guys?" He asked again and Reed just couldn't tell him anymore tonight and remarked "Good so far Ed, now get some rest tonight and we'll stop in tomorrow and check on you."

"Did you get a hold of Daisy?" He whispered before Reed could hang up.

"Yeah, she's okay." Reed looked at Jesse after hanging up. "We'll have to tell him tomorrow about his salesman."

Jesse wiped his brow on his napkin. "Yeah, I've got to go, but could you come along?"

"Sure thing. We can be sure it'll be in all the papers in the morning so we better get there early before someone else does and leaks the news of what went down." Reed tipped the last of his coffee from his cup and flagged down Flo for the check.

The town of Bemidji was a half hour away from Birch Lake and besides being a huge tourist attraction with its lakes and boutiques; it housed the biggest hospital facility for the northeast part of the state. Jesse had picked up Reed at seven thirty at the Woodsman again and they were on the road to see Ed and see what he could tell them about the shoot out the day before.

On the drive over, Reed brought Jesse up to speed. "I talked to Murph last night, and he said Daisy has moved to another part of town and that he would keep an eye on her."

"Good, she is safe then," Jesse remarked, relieved, "and I don't see how that maniac can find her now."

"Have you heard what time the Feds will hit town today?" Reed asked.

"Not till this afternoon, but I've got Elma on the door with orders to keep them out of my office, and she'll call me if I'm not back yet."

When they got to the hospital, Jesse parked the sheriffs' car in the lot for official vehicles and they hurried into the facility.

The minute they walked in the door, the smells hit them smack in the face. Reed recognized the odors of sickness, since it hadn't been that long since he had been laid up in one after getting shot working a case in Minneapolis. Now he tried not to breathe too deeply of the various odors as they stopped at the information desk and got the room number for Ed Harrison.

When they got to his room, they found him flat on his back with both legs encased in casts and attached to a contraption that held them in the air. Tubes and wires exited from his body as he lay sleeping.

"Goddamn," Reed whispered as he and Jesse stood quietly and gazed at their friend. "Should we wake him?" he said.

"God almighty," was all Jesse could say. But after a minute, he replied. "We better do it so he knows about his salesman and the other two."

"Christ, I'm awake. How the hell can I sleep like this?" He growled when he heard the two men whispering at his bedside. Then he fumbled and found the remote lying by his hand and pushed a button. "Christ," he moaned. "I need this dope." And he was quiet for a few minutes and they watched as his features quieted. "Now tell me--, what about my guys?" He asked.

Jesse stepped closer. "Ed, I'm sorry to say, Wally died. It was quick Doc says."

"That fucking bitch," Ed whispered. "And his poor wife and those kids." After a few minutes he was able to ask, "The others?"

"Your mechanic got a head wound, but is okay," Jesse hurried to say. "Not too serious but he lost a lot of blood. And his young helper was not hurt."

"Thank God for that." Ed closed his eyes. "The bitch left town then?" he asked.

"We can only hope, she wasn't sighted around Birch overnight." Jesse had called in help from the surrounding counties to patrol the town since his guys were here in Bemidji guarding the hospitalized men.

"Fuck, I can't believe that bitch could outdo four of us. How the hell did she manage to get my guys in that room?"

"Ed, try not to worry because you need to rest now. We're going to check on the mechanic," Reed said and started for the door. Ed could only nod his head. "Will you let me know what he says?" he asked weakly.

In the mechanic's room, the man sat in a chair and had a bandage on his head that looked like a football helmet. And when Jesse and Reed walked in, he tried to nod but winced at the movement. Jesse had known him for years as they had downed a few shots of whiskey together over time. Jesse asked him now, "Are you able to talk for a few minutes?"

A nurse came in then and ordered, "Do not stay more than five minutes and don't tire him out!"

"We promise," Jesse offered. When she had stepped out of the room Jesse turned to the mechanic. "Buddy, do you feel up to telling us what happened?"

"Yah, it was a woman, Jesse. Somehow she got my helper first and tied him up to a chair, then got him to call me to come into the lunchroom. I went in and stood there dumbfounded and in a flash, she had slipped handcuffs on me and said she'd kill my helper if I didn't get Wally in off the sales floor. When he came in, he flew at her to get the gun, but she just aimed and hit him. He went down and when I tried, she got me. I couldn't do anything to help. How could she do all that, four of us in just seconds?" The man leaned his bandaged head to the back of the chair and several minutes went by as his shoulders began to shake.

Reed and Jesse stood quietly and then Jesse put a comforting hand on his shoulder.

"Hey buddy, you did all you could." He said.

The mechanic sniffed and his voice weakened as he asked, "Did she get Wally then?"

"Yeah, sorry, Wally is dead, but we'll get her." Jesse exclaimed with a determined nod.

Just then a woman looking to be the mechanic's mother walked in and with a cry went to her son and leaned in close. Jesse and Reed stepped back.

"We'll be going now, but we'll come back later and check on you," Jesse said then and nodded to the woman.

The woman shook a fist in the air, "Sheriff, you better get who did this to my boy!"

Jesse nodded as he replaced his cap, "Yes, that is exactly what I'm working on right now!"

***

After getting that rushed message from Reed to get out of the hotel because the killer was on the way to Minneapolis and then tossing her things together, Daisy had hurriedly driven to the eastern outskirts of town to relocate. On the way she listened to Jesse's urgent message and then to a policeman called John Murphy, who gave Reed and Jesse as recommendations.

My God, she had breathed shakily as the messages clearly stated there was a 'new killer for hire' on her tail.

As she had gotten in her Porsche after leaving the hotel, she had laid her .38 by her side in the seat, taken the safety off and covered it with a scarf. This was war, and she would not be taken unawares. Reed had said this assassin was a female, and a striking looking one at that. Soon as she got settled in a new place, she would call him back and get a complete description of this person.

Daisy drove through the suburbs and then circled around to a new upscale motel located in Saint Paul and checked in. Here there was an enclosed garage to house her car within its concrete walls, and also on her way over, she had stopped and bought a throwaway cell so her calls could not be traced. Her thoughts were going a mile a minute as she locked her car and ran into the place through an enclosed ramp. Coming into the motel to the front desk, she slowed down and got her breath and looked around at the surroundings. Too bad she wouldn't have time to enjoy all of it as she especially loved the smell of newness, and the look of things fresh from its maker. She glanced at the overall colors that were black, brown and white with splashes of lime green accentuated in the room with accessories, pillows and matted art. Walking through the lobby, she saw a huge fawn colored sectional wrapped around a big rectangular coffee table, where a tall centerpiece of silk flowers towered in the center. Check-in was situated off to the side of the big room where muted phones rang and bells chimed in this busy enterprise.

Daisy checked in using a card, but then held out cash to pay in advance for her room.

"Now listen to me carefully," she said to the clerk. "I do not want my card to be listed anywhere on your records. This is for my identification only."

The clerk looked at her and shook her head. "I'm sorry, that's not how we do it."

Seeing this was going to be a difficult request, Daisy forced her already stressed out face into a smile and asked, "May I see your manager please?"

"Well I suppose," the clerk said, "I'll get him right away."

Again, Daisy had to explain that she did not want her card to be used in any way, and that she was paying in cash for her lodging. She instructed them not to put her name anywhere on their forms.

As she was standing there, impatience digging at her heels, for a minute she wondered if she told them the truth that a killer might be right on her heels ready to annihilate her, would they have understood her rush to get behind some doors? After all, for all she knew, this Ursula might be right behind her waiting to follow her to do just that in a room away from prying eyes. But then of course, if she told them that, they would have called the police and sent her away, anyway.

But finally, after another interval of precious time and their precious protocol, Daisy got a key and disappeared. However, not trusting them completely, she had reserved two rooms, for her guests, she had mentioned, just to make sure the killer couldn't know which one she would be in.

Oh, for God's sake, she whispered, if she weren't so damned tired she would have just kept on driving again after getting the "bums-rush" to get out of the Grand Hotel in downtown Minneapolis. However, maybe after a night's rest here, she would still do it tomorrow. She dropped her things in one of the rooms, turned on the television then slipped into the other room and did the same. Then she found a vending machine and bought water, coffee and numerous bars of junk so she wouldn't be seen out in the hallways and restaurants tonight, and finally she was able to sit down and call Reed back using her new cell.

"Okay Reed," she said in a tired voice, "I'm settled on the other side of town and on the way, I stopped and bought a throw-away cell phone to use as you recommended."

"Good to hear from you Daisy," Reed exclaimed. "Now be sure and call Billy Miller in the morning and let him know where you are too."

"Yes," she said. "But Reed, do you know how Ed is?" Daisy asked anxiously.

"I saw him this morning. He was shot in both knees so he is in pretty bad shape!"

"Oh, my God," Daisy whispered numb with sorrow.

"I'm sorry to lay this on you Daisy, but you need to know we have a ruthless killer on our hands. Wally,

Ed's salesman is dead. She shot the mechanic in the head, but he is okay. Totally shaken of course."

"What have I done," Daisy cried out then coming out of her silence.

"It's not your fault, Daisy, all this started when Roma Hurst tried to get away from this madman who followed her here from Norway."

"I know Reed, but then I got Ed involved and now he's terribly hurt. And his guys! Oh God." Daisy grabbed a tissue from a box on her bedside table, and for a minute she lost it and Reed patiently hung on the line. Then after a minute she got herself under control.

"Sorry Reed, I'm just so sorry, and scared." Then she whispered, "I'm okay now and you can call me at this new number on this cell."

"Okay, watch yourself Daisy, and even if you suspect someone is on to you, call 911 and also Murphy. And call me every day to let me know you're okay."

After that call she looked up the number for the hospital in Bemidji and found Ed. When she heard his pain-filled whisper, she felt even worse.

"Ed, this is Daisy. I'm so sorry you got hurt." She managed to say.

"Daisy," he said hoarsely, "Yeah, she got me."

"The pain is horrendous, I've heard. I talked to Reed a minute ago."

"Where the hell are you? Daisy, she's after you! She forced me. I had to tell her I thought you were at the

Grand in Minneapolis." Ed's voice shook as he whispered.

"I know Ed, but you had no choice. Reed found me and I have moved. Listen I've got a new cell number, a throw-away that doesn't record calls so I'll stay in touch every day."

"Okay," Ed said then, "Don't worry about me. Daisy, I've got 24 hour guards on my door so if she's still around here she won't get far."

"Be safe, I'll call tomorrow then," Daisy said, "And Ed, I'm so sorry I got you involved in my trouble."

"Daisy, I'll recoup, besides what are friends for?"

"Not to get shot at though." Daisy whispered unable any longer to keep the tears out of her voice.

"Listen Daisy, I'll be fine, and I might let you make it up to me when I get out of here."

After she clicked off the cell, she looked around the beautiful rooms but didn't feel anything but dread. The television was a flat wall screen, the furniture, a rich, ebony and again, the room had the same lime green accents. She tossed her clothes on the foot of the bed and slipped on a robe. Then she sat down at the desk and began to make her lists of things to do. Right now, after hearing the awful news from Reed, she was not in the right mood tonight to go forward with her plans for buying a home in the city.

She also got in touch with the company her old friend owned and asked her to postpone the plans to pack up her things and put her house on the market, for the next week or so, as there were situations that had come up that she needed to deal with first. She called her friend who owned the beauty shop next to her manicure business back in Birch Lake and told her some of the story.

"Luci," she said, "I'm sure you've heard what went on yesterday over at Ed's office. And that this maniac killed his salesman and hurt the other two guys."

Luci whispered. "I heard Daisy. Is it true this killer is a woman and is looking for you because you took her man?"

"No, nothing like that. Listen, I'm going to be away for a while, so will you kindly put a note on my door to the shop? And just to make sure you keep an eye on your people. If you see a suspicious looking stranger, call 911 and Jesse right away."

"Okay, Daisy," Luci said hesitatingly, "my husband just called and said I should close up and go home."

"Luci, I think you should too. Put a sign on your door too and leave right away." Daisy took a nervous breath. How in the world could she live with more people getting killed, all because of her!

After checking the locks again on her door, as she sat at the desk, a sudden crying whine got her attention. She looked around absent mindedly, then remembered Romeo whom she had tucked in her big purse hours ago when she had hurried out of the Grand Hotel. Of course over there as well as here, she had snuck him in.

Guiltily, she stepped over her suitcase and found Romeo, the little pile of rags and let the poor thing out. He sniffed and shook himself out, then gave her a soulful look, and lifted a leg and peed, right on the new carpet.

"Oh, for God's sake Romeo," Daisy exclaimed, "What do you expect from me, I've been busy getting us away from a crazed killer!" She mumbled as she took some of the hotels lovely towels and began sponging. "Now what do I do with you? I'm trying to hide out from this lunatic."

But Romeo only looked at her with his big brown eyes as he went and sat daintily on the purse and gently nosed it open further to see if there was any dinner in there for him. Finding only crumpled tissues he turned sad eyes to her again and sighed, putting his head down on his front paws. Then Daisy remembered the can of food she had tossed in one of her bags and jumped up and filled a saucer and then added water in one of the fine cups she had found next to a coffee maker. After he had eaten, she had no choice but to locate his leash and take him out to do his duty. She picked him up and put him back in her big purse and took a back elevator down and hurried outside around a corner to a copse of seedlings.

"Lord, if you don't get us killed Romeo, we'll be lucky," she whispered to him after a few minutes as she hurriedly stuffed him back in her purse and pulled a scarf around her face and hurried back to her rooms.

But just as she hurried into an elevator to get to her room on the fourth floor, she glanced at a lone woman who also got on, who seemed to look at her a little bit too long.

Daisy cringed and backed further into the corner.

Was this her? The woman who would kill her?

-10-

Jesse and Reed left the hospital in Bemidji after getting the report from Ed Harrison's guys. Wally had been killed, and the young helper was being treated in the psychiatric unit for Acute Stress Disorder. The third, who was the mechanic, had been shot in the head, but the bullet had just grazed his forehead, just missing killing him instantly. He had sat, pale and weakened, and told them in a whisper how it had all come down.

"It was a woman," he repeated, "A crazy woman!" His mother had sat there with him with a protective arm around his shoulders, and stood up after a few minutes and shooed Jesse and Reed out of the room. "He's had enough. Sorry, Jesse, he needs to rest now." So they were on their way back to Birch to continue with their search for clues to the identification of the woman and to assuage her damage to the town and its people.

"I'll have to check on Wally's family again and see what more I can do for them."

Jesse commented now as he drove the brown shiny LTD. "Christ, I'm glad his insurance was paid up, so those kids can go to college. Four of them, you know."

Reed shifted in his seat glad to take his mind off the awful crisis going on around him and commented. "I can't even fathom having that responsibility. That poor woman."

"God almighty, me either." And shaking his head sadly, Jesse said, "And I thought it was hell having to worry and put one kid through college, then get him to leave the nest finally and take care of himself."

"Yeah?" Reed said.

"How come you don't have any kids, Conners?" Jesse asked.

"Hmm-, guess I'm just not lucky enough." Reed said.

Jesse fumbled in his pocket and took out a cigar and lit up, then turned down his window halfway and Reed followed suit with a cigarette. Soon the car was white with smoke and they were both puffing away as they rehashed what they knew so far about the horrendous crime in their town.

Back in Birch Lake close to noon, they stopped in the Woodsmen Café to have breakfast and lunch. Jesse called Elma and found out the Feds were on their way and would be there in an hour.

"Is MacGreger coming along with them?" Reed asked.

"I haven't heard, but I hope so. He's the only one in that bunch of jerks that has any smarts."

Reed nodded his head in the affirmative. "Do you want me to come back with you?" He asked.

Jesse shook his head. "Thanks, but why don't you come in around one o'clock? I'll probably be ready to shoot them all if MacGreger isn't along."

"Good, I promised to check in with Lindy, but I'll come by after a while." And the two guys took leave of each other and went on about their business.

When Reed got back to his home on the lake, Lindy was sitting outside on the deck with a pile of suitcases standing by her. Her shiny silver Lexus was standing in the driveway.

"Lindy, you made the decision without me?" Reed asked after driving the Corvette in the garage and coming over.

Lindy Lewis had dressed in one of her new outfits; white pants and shirt with high-heeled white wedgies. Her hair had been cut into a classy wedge a few days ago and was a gleaming red. And after all her exercising she looked like a million.

He walked over to her and stood. He had thought this day would come again, but not this soon. After all their years together, he had felt the restlessness in her lately.

She smiled at him and said, "You know I make my own decisions."

"I should know that by now, Lindy. But maybe I've got something special to offer you!"

This got her attention and she sat up abruptly and asked, "What?"

"Hmm-," he teased, "Maybe I've been planning on something for us."

"Reed Conners," Lindy said swinging a sandaled foot, "You'd better tell me now and I hope it's something I like."

Reed lit a smoke. Should he confess to her his thoughts of wanting a family at last, and even marriage if she wanted it?" He sucked hard on the cigarette and tilted his head as these thoughts ran through it.

Could he see her with a youngster on her lap? Diapers in hand?

He stood silently and then frowned as the picture dimmed. And someone he didn't recognize replaced the image. What was that about? He was cemented to the spot, speechless. When he finally got his tongue back he said lamely, "Lindy, let's take a vacation and go away and you can pick the place! But you've got to give me some time right now as we're right in the middle of this huge murder investigation here!"

She was quiet and he saw her process this information with the changes on her face, and he knew her answer without her even saying a word.

"Reed, here's what I'll do. I will go ahead and look at possible areas and get back to you and we'll decide. Okay?"

With a sinking heart, he felt this might not happen. Well, maybe he needed some time too he thought defensively and said, "That's a deal Lindy. You let me know where you are and I'll meet you. Okay?" And they parted with an embrace and a long kiss. And soon Lindy was on the road and Reed went out to check on his boat, and then took it out for a spin.

After an hour he came back in off the water, stopped in his house for a shower and then went into town to the sheriff's office to see Jesse. As soon as he got there, right off, it didn't look good as a stranger was sitting at Jesse's desk and Jesse was pacing the floor. Reed went to his side.

"What the hell is going on," he asked in a raised voice. "Who is at your desk?"

Jesse's face was red as he nodded his head toward the interloper. "They sent out a new one, and he came in and just took over. Actually ordered me out of my seat, I almost hit the fucker! There's another one around here someplace."

"Goddammit," Reed swore. "MacGreger didn't come in?"

"Not yet anyway, I'm trying to locate him."

"Come on Jesse, let's go outside for a smoke and let the fuckers wonder what we're up to."

Outside they stood in plain view of the windows leading into the office.

Their black SUV stood at the curb with the usual blacked out windows. "They never hide their identity do they?" Reed commented nodding at the vehicle.

"Hell no," Jesse growled. "The minute they got in the door, the old dude who is sitting at my desk, ordered me to start talking. Everything you got," he ordered. "Not one friendly word about what I'd done so far. Does he think I'm just a small town nobody?"

"Nah, don't let the fucker get your goat, Jesse. We'll figure this out without him."

"Yeah?" Jesse blew out a cloud of cigar smoke.

"Listen Jesse, I had a thought on the way over. I remember Ed said this woman came to his party on his boat?"

Jesse looked at him with a smile. "Fucking A, her prints have got to be there all over the place,--unless she was smart." Taking out his cell, Jesse called the hospital in Bemidji and got Ed on the line. And after a short conversation, he got Ed's okay to board his vessel. "Look at the table by my bed downstairs and her glass should be there with mine," Ed shouted as he winced with pain.

Minutes later Jesse and Reed were over at Ed Harrison's place and walked down the dock to his boat. Locating the spare key, they boarded and opened the private lower level. It still held the stale remains of liquor and cigarettes.

"Looks like it needs a major airing out," Jesse mumbled as he walked into the huge bedroom/ living room. There on the bedside table stood several glasses, with cigarette butts in them. And Jesse carefully placed each one in plastic evidence bags and then found a small box to set them in. "Want to ride along Reed, let's head back over to the BOCA in Bemidji with these. Hopefully they've gotten a report back on that glass you brought over a few days ago.

"Sure," Reed said but his thoughts had gone back to the earlier meeting with Lindy. He was pissed at her. For Christ sake, how could she just up and leave him again?

Goddamn it, he thought, this is it! I'm not sitting around waiting to hear from her. This time, I'm done!

Lyn LaCoursiere

-11-

Daisy quickly looked away from the handsome woman on the elevator. The only description she had so far was that she was a good looking female. Could she be the "gun for hire" who would kill her behind closed doors?

Her heart jammed wildly in her chest as she pushed the stop and got off on second instead of fourth. The hair on the back of her head felt like it was standing on end as she stepped out. As the door slid closed, she saw she was alone.

She rushed for the stairs, and then suddenly reversed her direction. If this was the killer wouldn't she assume Daisy would do just that? Take the stairways?

She sucked in a breath and stood momentarily, undecided. Then she heard another elevator come to a stop on that floor and there wasn't anywhere to go, except, a nearby storage closet. She quietly slipped in and closed the door except for a small crack so she could see who was getting off.

With her eyes glued to the scene on second floor in the hotel in Saint Paul, Daisy didn't realize she was holding her breath until the elevator door opened and a couple of senior citizens stepped out. She let her breath out with a big swoosh and mumbled, "Oh crap!" She stepped out of the closet and got back on the elevator and punched the key for the fourth floor.

Safely back in her room, she slipped on her robe and settled in to watch a movie on television. After several hours she finally went to sleep in the big king size bed. She always needed extra pillows to bunch around herself and was burrowed in an undistinguishable pile of various feather filled ones as she slept soundly. In the still predawn hours of the night, she didn't hear the wisp of a card that was slipped into her locked door, but awoke instantly as she intuitively felt it open.

A moment of stunning silence followed and without waiting for a glimpse of whomever it was, Daisy jumped up out of bed and began to yell as loud as she could as she ran like hell for the door. Frantically grappling at it expecting to be grabbed from behind any second, she got it open, and it slammed against the wall as she ran down the hall screaming at the top of her lungs. As she tumbled down the hallway in her pj's a group of partying men got off the elevator just then and she ran right into their surprised arms.

"An angel from heaven," one said. "Look, sent right to me," one astonished barfly said.

"Nah, she wants me, look she's already ready for bed." Another proclaimed and pushed to get closer to Daisy.

As she stood enveloped within the group, in the melee that was taking place, whoever it was that had tried to get to her disappeared.

Daisy untangled herself from the rowdy bunch of partygoers. "Will you help me please, someone broke into my room! Did you see anyone running away?" She clasped her arms around her chest in an effort to control her trembling.

"Here little lady, sit down." One seemingly sober man helped her over to where a couple of couches were set in the hallway, and then motioned to another. "Hey Luey, you whiskey bum, call 911 to get help for this poor woman!"

Daisy's heart thumped wildly as she sat down and another guy stepped up. "Listen, you'll have to excuse my buddies, we're not all bad. We're all doctors interning here at the U, and this is our first night off this month." She glanced at his blond good looks and saw he could be about the same age as her sons.

Lyn LaCoursiere

"Take some slow breaths young lady," he said and knelt on the floor in front of her. "You're safe now," he said, "we'll stay with you until the police get here." And after several minutes she did feel better and was able to tell the police what had happened. She asked them to contact John Murphy. After he brought the police up to date on her problem, Murphy asked to speak to her. As his voice came on the line, he introduced himself, saying he had known Reed and Ed for years.

"Here's what I'm going to do Daisy," he went on to say. "I've ordered twenty-four hour guards outside your hotel room door, and I need you to please stay inside until further notice from me."

"Okay," Daisy could only whisper. Going back to her room, she tried to catch some sleep but to no avail. Now she was a prisoner in her own room, so she showered and called room service for coffee and lots of it and then ordered food. Now all she could do was sit, wait and eat.

Her world was in a mess. She couldn't go home because her lovely house in Birch Lake could be still infested with those awful dangerous snakes and her business would soon be in ruins since she couldn't be there to take care of it. All because of her relationship with Roma and her boyfriend. Who, by the way were both dead!

For the rest of the night, Daisy paced around the hotel room, and then remembered she had to get in touch with her attorney, Billy Miller, today. As soon as it got to be a decent time she used her cell and called his office. When she was connected with him, he told her he had some good news and asked if she could meet him for lunch.

"I can't leave here, Mr. Miller. It'll have to be some time later." Daisy whispered.

"Okay. When would it be more convenient for you?"

Daisy lit a cigarette. She'd had several during the long night so far and lit up again. Damn, she had the bathroom exhaust going full blast, so what more could she do? This was war! Then because she was so overwrought, she babbled on.

"Mr. Miller. I don't know you very well yet, but I may as well tell you, I can't leave my hotel room because I have a 'killer for hire' after me. I have a cop outside my door right now."

In his business, Billy Miller had dealt with crooks and shysters, liars and murderers, and hadn't met one yet that intimidated him.

"Miss O'Dell, I can't imagine how you could have gotten yourself in such trouble. Reed Conners brought me up briefly last week when he called me before you came down."

Daisy swallowed over the lump of fear that threatened to take her breath away.

"How about if I come there, I have some papers I need you to sign."

Butterflies amok in her stomach, she wondered, could she trust this Billy Miller? John Murphy had said, "Don't let anyone in your room!" But Miller was an officer of the court, someone above suspicion. So she quickly agreed.

As Daisy waited in her hotel room alone, worried at every little creak and rattle she heard coming through the walls, she had to admit, she was scared.

But she was lonely, and at a low point of confidence. She hadn't felt this blue since dealing with her divorce years ago. There was no one in her life that cared about her. No one that loved her or that she could love. Over the ten years she had been single, she'd had several men in her life, but no one that she truly loved, and now in this moment of restlessness and horror, she wanted to break out and scream at the top of her lungs at her predicament.

But she forced herself to calm down, and showered and dressed in a lime green linen dress, swished her blonde hair in a careful fluff and liberally spritzed Prada cologne on herself. As she was getting ready to see the attorney, she suddenly felt a quickening of her heartbeat at the thought of his handsomeness, and remembered the interest she had seen flicker in his eyes as Reed had introduced her. And she had to admit, it had caused a little bit of excitement to flash through her thoughts as well. Now as a knock resounded on her door, she peeked out and saw the security guard, and her breath caught in her throat as she saw Billy Miller standing beside him, briefcase in hand.

She opened the door, and stepped aside.

"Hello, Miss O'Dell," he said, "I just need you to sign a paper. It's a consent agreement to proceed from the Hurst attorney."

She stepped aside holding the door, and then thanked the security guard.

"First of all, call me Bill, and if it's okay I'll call you Daisy," he said setting down his briefcase on the coffee table. He took out a file and opened it to the page for her to sign. That done, he grinned and took out a gift wrapped package. "Then I always like to give a new client this." And he handed it to her.

Taken by surprise, Daisy opened it and found a bottle of Heidseick champagne.

"Thank you, I see this could become one of my favorites," She exclaimed when she saw the expensive label. "Should I open this now?" She asked.

"If you would like, but let me do it for you." He popped the cork. "Do you have any glasses?" He asked.

Minutes later as the bubbly worked its magic on Daisy's nerves, she began to relax and the world didn't look so black, so troublesome, and she returned his easy smile as they talked.

"Are you single and in a relationship?" He asked her thirty minutes later and she replied that she was single and not in a relationship.

"And, may I ask, are you?" Daisy asked him.

With a catch in his voice he said, "I lost my wife to cancer years ago."

For a minute Daisy didn't know just how to respond, then she collected her thoughts. "I'm so sorry Bill." She reached over and touched his arm, then asked, "Do you have children?"

He smiled then nodding his head, "I do. I have three girls and they're all in college."

"Wow," Daisy lifted her glass. "Three girls," she repeated. "I can't imagine how that must feel."

"Well, let me tell you, sometimes I just want to give them all back. They live in a dorm and go to the U of M. This year the oldest one will be graduating with her masters in business. The next two are studying law."

"Do you have kids?" Bill asked then.

"I do, I have two sons." Daisy remarked. "They are grown now, of course, and live out of state.

"Let me congratulate you, Daisy. I'm learning it takes a patient and resourceful parent to see them through all the pitfalls of growing up."

"Money too," Daisy added.

"Yup, tons of that!" And they both laughed.

By now, as Daisy talked freely to Billy Miller, with the aid of the champagne, she could feel the electricity in their attraction.

She wondered, would an affair with him be as exciting as it felt right now?

-12-

As Reed rode with Jesse, Birch Lake's Sheriff to Bemidji to personally bring the evidence to the BOCA, the Bureau of Criminal Apprehension headquarters office, Reed's cell vibrated. Answering it, Murphy hastily brought him up on what had transpired during the early morning hours down in Minneapolis with Daisy.

"Goddamn, these people are intent on getting her. Where is she now?" Reed asked.

"She is tucked in with guards outside her door," Murphy told him.

"I just couldn't understand how they could find her so easily in the past, John," Reed exclaimed. "But here's a thought I had last night, no one has looked for a GPS on her car. That's got to be how they can find her! A tracking device!"

"Aw- hell," Murphy mumbled. "I'll get my men on it."

"Let me know what you find." And Reed hung up and brought Jesse up on what took place earlier that day in Minneapolis. When they got to the bureau, they were also advised that no prints in their files matched the ones on the glass Reed had brought over earlier.

Elma, Jesse's desk girl called him on the ride back to Birch and told him MacGreger from the FBI had just gotten there.

"Tell him to shoo that goon away from my desk and keep the seat warm for me. I'll be there in forty-five minutes."

He grinned at Reed. "Now we'll get something done," he said as he stepped on the gas in the shiny brown LTD

Getting back to Birch Lake, when they walked into Jesse's office, the place seemed dwarfed by the three FBI men. As Jesse approached his desk, Tom MacGreger stood up and the men shook hands.

"Good to see you, Tom," Jesse said. "You remember Reed Conners, don't you? He's working with me on this case. Pull up some chairs and we will bring you up to date." Jesse had no choice but to include the other two FBI agents as well.

"Now here's what's gone on so far," and Jesse went on to elaborate how Gunther Mueller had Roma followed to the US, Daisy shooting him and then the threatening individuals that followed.

"How safe is the place, she's in?" Tom MacGreger asked. The man looked the same as he had back when he had first come to Birch Lake with the FBI and helped sort out the issues about Lindy Lewis when she had been jailed as an accomplice with drug lord, Mario D'Agustino. His dress was casual and not in the customary blue suit, white shirt and red ties as the other men. Instead of a buzz haircut, his was shaggy and unruly. He wore the same horn-rimmed glasses and had an easy smile.

Reed sat off to the side and just nodded his head in agreement from time to time. He hadn't wanted to interfere with their conversation but now he wanted in. MacGreger had just suggested he would go down to Minneapolis and join up with John Murphy. The other two FBI men could stay there and keep an eye on Birch Lake.

"I would like to join up with you Tom, I know John Murphy well and I'm sure he would like all the extra help." Reed suggested.

Tom MacGreger looked at Reed and agreed. And within a few more minutes the meeting was over with Tom agreeing to meet Reed at the downtown precinct in Minneapolis in several hours.

"Okay, Tom, I just need to stop home and grab a few things and I'll be on the road. And Jesse, I'll keep you up on what we run into down there." Reed hurried out of the sheriff's office and sped home. He called his neighbors, Abby and Joe, to let them know he would be gone.

"I'm not sure how long but at least a few days. However, I'll call, Abby," he said to her. In his bedroom, he opened a suitcase and threw in underwear and socks, toiletries, slacks, shirts and a sport coat, then locked up the house. As he drove out of the yard, he stopped and got out, and pulled the big wooden gate across the road which he had installed recently and padlocked it. He left it open when he was at home, but now, no one could drive into his place while he was gone. Tourists sometimes seemed to find their way down his private twisting road, through the woods, too often. He finally got pissed after finding a group of strangers fishing off his dock one day when he came from town.

It was going on one o'clock on a Wednesday afternoon when he settled into the three hour drive to Minneapolis. MacGreger had called ahead and talked to John Murphy and said he and Reed were on their way to give him a hand.

It had been several years since Reed had found Murphy's wife, Annie, safe in that old Grain Belt building down there after being kidnapped by that sociopath called Wolff. He'd been close friends with the Murphy family and was Godfather to their two little girls. Murphy had invited him over one night for dinner while he was in town too.

"Okay, here's where we are so far," Murphy said later as the three men sat in his office. "You were right, we found a GPS tracking device attached to Daisy's Porsche. We left it there. Now we'll just wait for him or her, to show up at her hotel room." Reed asked. "Are you sure she's safe at that same place?"

"My men are taking turns 24/7 at her door."

"Murphy, we don't have a description, and we don't know if it's a he or a she this time." MacGreger added.

"We'll soon find out." John Murphy shook his head. "Usually takes only a day or two and something will happen."

"Tom and I will go over and check the place out," Reed stood up, "and I'll call you, Murph."

"Good, I need to finish up some paperwork here and then I'll join you over there at say, six o'clock? And, we have to be very careful and not let him see us." John Murphy waved them out and picked up his ringing phone receiver.

MacGreger left his rental in the parking lot by the police station and jumped in the Corvette with Reed.

"Sure you don't want to get rid of this ride?" He asked, looking around inside the luxury car.

"You shopping around for this model?" Reed shifted into second gear as they went down the drive in the parking ramp.

Tom MacGreger laughed. "I collect them."

"No shit, how many you got?" Reed gave him an interested look.

"Hm--, maybe around a dozen."

"A dozen vette's, are you nuts?" Reed laughed too.

"My wife says so," MacGreger added.

"Tom, what the hell do you do with a dozen Corvettes?"

"I'm a mechanic at heart, Reed. I buy old junked ones and fix them up. I live on a farm with a huge garage where I tinker with these pieces of "junk" as my adored wife calls them."

"I'll be damned Tom, I never figured you for a "Garage Geek." Reed said as he moved into a fast lane and they took off for the hotel where Daisy was at.

"Well, it keeps me sane." Tom took out a cigarette after he saw Reed light up.

"I just take my boat out and stay for a while. Sometimes days," Reed confessed as he put his window down a few inches so his smoke blew out. Tom did the same on his side of the car.

"I've often wondered Reed, what ever happened to Lindy Lewis. You know, I really liked that woman even though she seemed to be a little on the flaky side."

Reed laughed. "Then my friend, you wouldn't be surprised to learn she just up and left Birch a few days ago."

"Yeah? You two been together then?"

"Well mostly. But after all the D'Agustino notoriety, she moved to Mexico." Reed said and shook his head.

"Really."

"Yup, just up and left the country then too." Reed said. "But it wasn't long before she got in trouble and I bailed her out, again."

"You really are hooked on her, aren't you, my friend?" MacGreger shook his head and laughed.

"It would seem so." Reed admitted dryly. He took a deep drag on his Marlboro and tossed it out the window as they raced through the congested downtown traffic over to Saint Paul and Daisy's hotel.

"Go ahead Bill and get comfortable," Daisy urged Billy Miller and he had stood up and had taken off his suit jacket, unbuttoned his shirt collar and loosened his tie. "Thank you, I appreciate this, Daisy. I've been in this since seven this morning when I had an early meeting."

"You sound like a busy guy," Daisy went on to say. "I am usually busy too, or I should say, was, until all these things started happening."

"Tell me more about your friend, Roma Hurst. How long had you known each other?" Bill asked. And Daisy told of their meeting years ago in the cul-de-sac, their young married life with husbands and raising their kids.

"And we both wound up divorced," Daisy went on to say.

"Did you stay in touch with each other over the years?" He asked.

"Off and on and then we'd catch up." Daisy sipped the last of her champagne and put her glass down carefully on the coffee table. She felt a little tipsy, but it also felt good because the small knot of terror she'd had in the pit of her stomach for days seemed to have disappeared. She smiled at the relief.

"Should I pour another glass for you? If you say yes, I'll have another too," Billy announced then with a grin on his handsome face. And feeling so much better, Daisy could only agree.

"Listen to this," she murmured and laid her head back on the top of the couch and closed her eyes for a minute as a song by Norah Jones came on the stereo. He refilled their glasses as they listened to the music.

"We need to toast our new found friendship," He said holding up his champagne glass.

"Good idea, here's to a fulfilling time." They clinked glasses, and he leaned over and gave her a quick kiss on her lips.

Daisy blinked, then smiled. "Hey, that tasted good!" And he reached for her glass and placed it with his on the coffee table, then put his arm over her shoulder and gently pulled her closer.

"Damn," he said. "You taste good too!" She recognized his Armani cologne.

Soon their kisses went deeper and got hotter. By now, Daisy was completely caught off guard at her own reaction. A little voice inside her whispered, slow down, you've only just met the man, and here you are, ready to toss your clothes and dash to the nearest bed with him! She untangled herself from his embrace but stayed close.

"Let's sit for a while," she managed to whisper, "and enjoy the music with our champagne." They listened to more of the songs on the CD Daisy had bought while shopping one day.

But after only a few, it still didn't slow down their feelings or his action. And Billy Miller just scooped her up in his muscular arms as they hungrily found each other again in a deep kiss. He laid her down on the king sized bed just across the room.

He unbuttoned her dress and slid it down over her chest, then unsnapped the lacey front of her bra and found a rosebud nipple and kissed one, then the other.

Daisy held him to her breast as her rapture sent rivulets of pleasure clear down to her toes. After a time, he slipped her dress down over her knees and tossed it aside. Then put his fingers inside her lacey bikini underwear and began to massage her as he kissed her belly. Then she felt his hot lips move on down and she wanted every moment of it, as she lay, relaxed and open for his love.

Time flew by and she soon climaxed amid the chaos of her thoughts. Billy sat up and threw off his clothes, then pulled her on top of him and they soon were joined, absolutely enjoying each other again. Over and over, throughout the night, their attraction was electric and their love explosive.

-13-

Daisy sat up and gazed at the man sprawled out in her king size, hotel bed and wondered, now why did I do this? Outside of being a little drunk on that wonderful champagne, I don't usually get into this kind of situation, clandestine or otherwise, with anyone. Especially a new acquaintance.

She lay her head back down on the starched pillowcase and thought about that as she stared at the ceiling and brushed a hand over her eyes. Her thoughts rambled, this man was a great lover, but would he be just as exciting to see every day and again every night, in bed? She'd have to think more about this. Just then, Billy Miller woke up.

"Hey beautiful," he murmured, and pulled her into his arms. She stiffened slightly and he felt her instant restraint. "What's wrong?" He asked.

Daisy rose up on an elbow and pulled the sheet over her chest. "Hmm-," she murmured, "I'm shocked at myself for what I've done."

"Why, what did you do" he asked. "You're sorry we spent the night together?"

"Well, yes." Daisy sat up again and brushed her hair back and away from her face. Then she went on, "I don't mean you, Bill, I loved what we had together. I mean here the guards are outside my door staying up all night and I'm in bed having sex with my attorney, for God's sake."

Billy Miller smiled and moved the sheet a bit and ran a finger over a nipple. "Well, I bet they wished they were as lucky as me."

Daisy had to smile too. "Damn, but now I'm sure I've ruined my reputation."

"I suppose now your parents will make us get married too." He joked and Daisy found she liked his kidding and his light banter. Then sitting up, reaching for her robe and tying it around herself as she stood, she remarked.

"I need coffee and lots of it. How about you? Do you eat breakfast?"

"Yes and yes." Billy said as he stood up in all his glory.

"Hmm-," a pleasing murmur escaped Daisy's lips before she clapped a hand over her mouth, then laughed.

"Okay lady, if I didn't need to be on my toes in court early this morning, I would do something about you again. But for now, may I use your bathroom for a shower, then I can go right into my office. I have a change of clothes there for emergencies."

"And I will order room service." After doing that, she opened her door and peeked out. Two guards turned to her when they heard it open. Daisy cleared her throat. "Everything quiet out here?" she asked.

"Yes," they said and nodded.

"Listen guys, I have ordered room service. Knock when it gets here."

"Yes ma'am." Then the other one chimed in, "We've done this before."

"Sorry," Daisy managed to answer, totally embarrassed. She closed the door quickly.

Billy came out of the bathroom with a towel tied around his waist. "I found the toothbrush and deodorant you set out for me. Thank you, although now, I 'spose since I smell so girlie from your soaps, I'll have the gays fighting over me." He laughed as he slipped into his clothes.

Daisy had ordered up coffee, juice and toast and they ate their breakfast at the table the server had pushed in and listened to the news on the TV.

It was going to be a clear fall day with warm temps, and some humidity, the radio announcer predicted.

Lyn LaCoursiere

Traffic was moving at a fast pace and the weekend was approaching with speed he went on to say. "Soon Halloween will be here and then we have the holiday season coming up. This year, make it special for that loving person in your life and give diamonds. Guys, it's a girl's best friend!"

Daisy had slipped on a rose colored short robe earlier and while Billy was in the shower, quickly stepped in and brushed her teeth and her hair. Without any make-up on, she really did look like a boy. So much like one of her boys actually, but with a few wrinkles. And like each of them too, a light sprinkling of freckles across the bridge of her nose.

The attorney leaned across the table. "Tell me, can I see you tonight, Daisy?" He asked.

Daisy smiled. "As long as you bring the champagne and make love to me like you did last night, you can see me every night." Oh Lord, she thought to herself, what made me say that? I'm not ready for anything like this now, of all times! For God's sake, I'm trying to outrun a killer, and I'm homeless. "And what about Ed?" Daisy didn't realize she had murmured this out loud.

"Ah-humn," Bill cleared his throat and commented dryly, "And, who is Ed, competition maybe?"

Daisy was immediately brought back to reality. "Ed is a good friend who lives in Birch Lake, and he put his life on the line to save me. He's in a hospital right now back there, after almost getting killed."

"Are you in a relationship, or wanting to start one with him?" Billy asked. "I don't want to come between you two if you do?"

"No," Daisy shook her head. "It's not a good time for me to plan on anything right now."

Billy Miller glanced at his watch. "Daisy, I'm sorry, I need to take off, but let's talk about this more. Can I call you at the noon break?" And he hurriedly kissed her and was gone in seconds.

After he left, Daisy sat and put her chin on one hand and toyed with her coffee cup with the other. Wow, she'd spent most of the night making love with this handsome man and right off she felt as if she was falling in love with this stranger.

How could that be? She had been there before but this time it felt different. She frowned and her brow wrinkled as she puzzled at this. Well, one thing she realized, she smiled a lot with him. There was something about his eyes. That looking into his, promised her envisions of happiness and lovely secrets to share with him. A look she hungrily needed to fill a lonely place in her heart.

The joy of it, she murmured, then raised the cup of coffee to her lips but thought, If only life was easy.

Her cell phone chimed a cheerful good morning and startled her out of her reverie of thoughts. Reed Conners' voice came over the line.

"Glad to hear you're sounding chipper today, Daisy. How was your night?"

She smiled to herself and replied, "Good, thank you Reed."

"I just wanted you to know that I'm here in Minneapolis, in fact right here in your hotel."

Oh no, she thought, does he know that the attorney he introduced me to a few days ago, spent the night in my bed? Her cheeks actually felt hot. But she went on and asked, "Where are you?"

"I'm in the coffee shop. John Murphy is here too with an FBI agent."

"Really," Daisy replied swallowing slowly. "The FBI?"

"Yes. Daisy, we're dealing with assassins from across the pond, so that makes it their business too."

"Okay," she answered lamely. "But Reed, my God, this whole thing is getting bigger not better."

"Don't get upset Daisy. We have a plan and we should have it wrapped up tonight."

Well, that certainly was good news, but would that mean she would be locked up here for another day?

And sure enough, he went on, "But we need you to stay in today and tonight so we know you are safe here with the guards." Reed said.

But he didn't dare tell her about the GPS the killer had and knew exactly where she was at all times.

-14-

The three men, Reed, John Murphy and MacGreger, from the FBI had gathered in the lounge at the hotel where Daisy was staying, late that evening and had hastily drawn up a plan. Murphy had called in extra men from his department, the Minneapolis Police Department, and during the night they all took turns watching the entrance and exit doors at the hotel. Not that they knew what Daisy's suspected assassin looked like, but they checked ID's from every single one coming and going in the place. Several customers complained they would never come back to this Saint Paul landmark after this intrusion, but mostly the customers were appreciative of the tight surveillance the hotel had for its customer's safety. Now this morning, after an uneventful night the three men gathered again in the coffee shop to plan for the day.

"I talked to the GM on the way in," Reed said now to them. "The hotel is expecting a busy check-in between 9:00 and 12:00 noon today for the annual antique car show that starts this afternoon in the courtyard. Over fifty vehicles will be shown, and hundreds of people are expected to come through."

"Man, it's going to be impossible to keep the lid on this now," MacGreger added and the group was silent for a moment.

Murphy wiped his forehead on his napkin. "Here's what I would like to do, let's get Daisy out of here and to a safe house. Then at least, whoever this is, if he or she gets past us, we won't have to worry about her safety."

"Good idea, goddamn, she isn't going to like it, but I'll talk to her." Reed grinned then, "Although, she should be in a good mood this morning, after her all night company."

"Uh ha," Murphy agreed and shook his head. "Miller is one of the best attorneys around town, but that mouth piece is known as quite the pussy hound among his peers."

The guys chuckled at that then got serious again. They took out their cells and all began making arrangements for the day.

When Daisy answered her cell, she asked worriedly, "Reed, what's going on? Have you arrested anyone?"

"Nope, a quiet night and morning, but here's what I need to talk to you about. The hotel is expecting a heavy check-in this morning and a busy day and we're worried about keeping track of all the strangers coming in. Murphy wants you to go to a safe house for a while."

Daisy huffed out a breath, then murmured, "Really?"

"Yup. Sorry about the inconvenience Daisy, but I feel you should."

"For how long?" She asked impatiently and put her coffee cup down with a bang.

"Not long. Sorry," Reed said again. "We're trying to keep you alive Daisy."

"Oh crap, I'm sorry Reed. I guess my nerves are getting the best of me again."

"Okay then, I'll call you back in a few minutes." She hung up and looked around quickly noting all the things she would have to pack up again and mumbled, "Oh crap," again.

A few minutes later Reed called back, "Daisy, in ten minutes MacGreger will come by and get you. Grab a suitcase with things you'll need for the next few days."

"Okay Reed, where will I be going?" Daisy asked.

"Not on the phone, just in case." Reed commented. "Trust me, he'll explain it to you on the way."

So here it was again. Daisy had to run again for her life. When would it ever stop? Would whomever it was out there trying to kill her, be caught this time?

By noon, she was settled in her new home, and from what MacGreger explained it was heavily guarded. She would be safe!

Now also close to noon, the three men rendezvoused for several minutes at the hotel. Since discovering the GPS on Daisy's Porsche which stood in the hotel ramp, and thinking it would eventually lead the killer right into their hands, as yet, nothing had transpired in the last night and this morning.

"Let's not get impatient, guys," MacGreger reminded Reed and Murphy. "Remember, he's got to be getting pretty tired of this too!" So, they all agreed. "But let's get together again at say, around 4:00." And the men went back to their posts taking turns waiting and watching for Daisy O'Dell's would be killer.

At three forty-five, the Saint Paul hotel was jumping with action. Hundreds of people mulled around the shiny renovated old cars with their proud owners standing guard. Men were stationed again at the entrance and exit doors checking ID's. Reed and Murphy were manning the elevator doors in the lobby and MacGreger and his man were stationed on fourth floor, watching Daisy's door into her old room.

As Reed and Murphy were busy with families laden with suitcases and bags, and amid the confusion of the teeming lobby, a uniform clad man carrying a tool case hurried into a waiting elevator. Major Elevator Company was stitched on the back of his shirt.

Reed's breath caught. "Did you see him?" He yelled to Murphy over the melee of rushing people and nodded in the direction of the elevator Murphy was watching.

Murphy's head turned toward it as the door swished closed.

"Shit," Murphy yelled. "Goddamn," Reed cussed and they both ran for the stairway that was just around the corner.

Taking two and more steps at a time they both ran up the four flights of stairs and came crashing through the door onto Daisy's floor. They gave MacGreger a heads up and the men slipped behind empty room doors to wait and watch.

Time stood still as they calmed their breathing and remained quiet. Nothing happened for what seemed like an hour, then they watched as this same man silently hurried out of the elevator, went up to Daisy's door and slipped something in the lock. Inside of ten seconds he was inside and closed the door. Immediately, the men also quietly opened her door. They stepped inside with guns ready, to an empty room. Reed nodded toward the bedroom, and just then they heard shots and he sent the door crashing into the wall. The surprised assassin turned at the sound, and she was met with three gun barrels pointing straight at her head.

Lyn LaCoursiere

-15-

Ursula Arickson grew up on the streets of Oslo. She never knew her parents and never stayed long enough in orphanages and foster homes to feel the warmth and love of a caring home. At thirteen years old, she ran away from the system and became a prostitute and at sixteen she had had two abortions, and born a daughter. She lived in one room in a warehouse and squirreled her hard earned money away under a floor board under her bed. And to save even more, she never ate more than one meal a day. If she was lucky, she could make the trip through her working area in time to find some food the bars put out to feed their customers. Ursula worked alone and didn't dare stay around too long in any of the bars, because if the owners knew she was picking up their customers, they would expect a cut of her money or they would call the police on her and she would be arrested. This way, she was in and out and she had gotten so good at her work she could cull out the wishful wage earners and connect with the big spenders in a matter of minutes.

Ursula was a natural blonde but darkened her hair to a rich auburn. Her eyes were brilliant blue and even though she had never eaten a healthy diet, she was fortunate to have a clear cameo complexion. She was five foot five inches tall and weighed 135 pounds. Her dresses were all short and her feet always encased in three inch stiletto heels. Little by little, over the years she moved up to nicer neighborhoods in Bergen and began to frequent nicer bars for her business. By now, she was known by the most of the constabulary's but just to make sure she was staying in good graces with police, she would give "freebies" from time to time.

When she was twenty, an interesting ad in a newspaper caught her eye. She read and reread the mysterious words which sounded very intriguing to her. She answered it and after countless interviews, she was hired. She was to be ready to travel at any given time, but needed to change her appearance to look more like a successful lady. The starting pay was five thousand a month and greatly more then she made at that time. After another phone call, she was invited to also meet a gentleman behind this mysterious business. So one of the first things she did was give herself a personal overhaul, and after a day in a spa, she stepped out coiffed and smartly dressed. And tonight, Ursula dressed in one of her new outfits and brushed her richly colored auburn hair into the wedge look she had instantly liked. She had been to the Upstairs Eating Emporium several times before with one of her clients. But tonight she had almost a real date at this private and very elegant restaurant. She was to be ready at eight 0'clock and a car would pick her up and upon arrival, she was to ask for Mr. X. Well, this was too good to be true; making big money, for doing nothing and then being treated like this.

Ursula walked into the restaurant and could feel the interested looks from the men as she stood waiting to be shown to the man's table. And she liked it; this richness which gave her license to be there. She had arrived at last, she felt.

She followed the maitre'd through a crowded dining room to Mr. X's table. He stood up and offered his hand, saying, "So, my man was right when he said 'you'd fit the bill.'"

It took Ursula only a few minutes to size him up. He was elegantly dressed in a black casual tux and his graying hair had an expensive cut. He was trim and slim, tanned and his hands looked well cared for. Apparently, he had never worked a hard day in his life, she saw right off. His English was perfect too, she heard, without any trace of his heritage.

"May I call you Ursula," he asked as the maitre'd held her chair and she sat down.

"Certainly, and what shall I call you Mr. X," she asked as she leaned down and adjusted her hemline, and just enough, as tonight, she was wearing a purple satin dress that fit her slim body in just the right places. She had been blessed with an ample chest which served her nicely in her business and she displayed it wantonly whenever she felt the time was right. And, tonight seemed really right.

Taking his eyes off her bosom, he answered without a pause, "You can call me Jonas." Then the table was surrounded with waiters with iced water, a magnum of champagne in a bucket of ice, and menus.

Now Ursula had been a working girl since running away from that last family and was not used to such great opulence, but she had a fantasy of meeting a prince someday who would take her away from the life she had been forced to develop. And tonight of all nights, could be interesting she saw. The man was good-looking, apparently rich and maybe he was single.

"I wanted to meet you, and as my man promised, 'I would be delighted.'" As he spoke, the waiter poured their glasses of champagne and they raised them now in a salute. He smiled as they clinked their glasses. And feeling that finally, she was about to raise her lifestyle level after meeting this grandiose man, she returned his smile.

MOONBEAMS TOO 131

"You are a lovely woman, my dear," he went on to say. "Tell me what kind of work you have been involved in?"

Ursula raised her chin and spoke smoothly, "I'm a valued officer in the Lutheran Church offices right here in Bergen."

"In administration I'm sure," Jonas commented. "You look to be very capable in that field."

"Well, thank you, I've been in that work for years now." Ursula lifted her glass of champagne and took a bigger drink then she was ready for and almost choked on it.

"I recognized the address my driver picked you up at, have you lived there long?" He asked.

"Oh yes," Ursula murmured telling another tale, actually she had just rented rooms last week in the classy neighborhood. "For years, I was raised just blocks from where I live now." She thought her voice sounded sexy.

"Lovely area." Jonas remarked.

"Where do you live?" She dared to ask.

"Well now, I like to move around. Sometimes in other areas." The man smartly avoided her question and adjusted the links in his French cut shirt.

Ursula hoped her eyes hadn't bulged when she saw those were real diamonds in his shirt cuffs. Well, if they were, she could match those, and she laid her right hand on the table where she was sure he would see her diamond rings. Which by the way, she had taken very discreetly, from that bitch she had met with last month on that so called threesome.

Their waiter came over then and asked if they were ready to order dinner. And Jonas did the honors. "I'm sure you will love my selections," he said and leaned in and brushed her cheek with his lips.

Well now, things were moving along. Ursula felt by the end of the evening she would have him literally kissing her somewhere else. And she enjoyed the seafood he ordered and the lovely braised calf. During dinner they drank both a velvet white wine and a smooth tasting Cabernet, and topped it off with an after dinner brandy.

When Jonas suggested she come back to his place to see his hunting trophies she was thoroughly toasted, and could see he was falling for her charms to be sure, as she had never been treated to such lovely food and drink.

Awakening later in a strange bed, she sat up and looked around at this opulence. That was the start of the affair, but it ended abruptly in a few weeks later when Ursula killed a burglar in self-defense, she thought, but was charged with murder. When Jonas refused to give her an alibi unless she joined his special services, which was a "killer for hire" service she realized she was framed, and had no choice, otherwise she would go to prison. These services were available only to the very rich and noble upper class of the European and Asian countries. Unbeknownst to Ursula, Jonas was a cousin and another family member of the famous boat building company located in Oslo, Norway. After Gunther Mueller, Bjorn and his sister Astrid had been annulated by the crazy "merkins" in the US, now the rest of the family had gotten involved and was furiously out for revenge.

And today Amelia Arickson had come face to face with the devils who held their gun barrels pointed directly at her heart. Would her certain death be the end of the hunt?

Lyn LaCoursiere

-16-

The exact timing was stunningly swift as the three men, Reed, MacGreger, and Murphy flew into action and faced the killer in Daisy's hotel room with their guns pointed directly at her head. Her actions were lightning fast, as well, but in the seconds it took her to spin around to find her target, they had already found theirs.

The three had discussed it earlier and decided to take the shooter alive, if at all possible. That once and for all, they would have some leverage in getting to the bottom of this endless shooting spree, that some overseas autocrat had in for one of their US citizens.

In those seconds too, Reed had gotten close enough to the assassin holding a Glock, and when he smacked her hand, it went flying through the air like a piston shot from a cannon.

"Oh----," the woman groaned and fell to the floor clutching her wrist. He pointed his Colt 38 at her head again as Murphy jammed a pair of cuffs on her. MacGreger read her, her rights and they had taken her down the elevator in minutes and out a side exit to a police car where she was locked in.

"Goddamn," Reed exclaimed as the three men gathered for a minute and took some deep breaths to get a grip on their actions.

"Okay," Murphy said, "My guys will take her downtown but let's leave her sweat overnight in a cell. Do you want to meet back tomorrow?"

"Can't keep me away," Reed said and McGreger joined in with, "Or me!"

"What all can we hold her on now?" Reed asked.

"Breaking and entering first of all, and you can be sure that Glock is not registered to her!" Murphy wiped a hand over his forehead. "And I'll come up with more, but we need to concentrate on finding out who runs the show across the pond."

"Well, good luck with it guys. Something like this, it's usually so deeply hidden we'll never find out." MacGreger shook his head.

"We could arrest her for attempted terrorism and threaten her with the chair." Reed added.

"Ahh--," McGreger began and shook his head. "Then she would pull the Patriots Act on us and the case would instantly be hidden in courts for years. And, I've learned if captured, they will go to that chair before they will give up any information." MacGreger lit a cigarette. "They're cold-blooded as hell!"

"Okay, let's take a break and let her stew in a cell. Meet me tomorrow then in my office around noon and we'll go from there." And the guys went to their cars and left the area; Murphy to his office in the downtown police precinct. MacGreger, to the FBI headquarters, and Reed to catch up with friends at Gina's Café in downtown Minneapolis. He was tired after a long day of watching and waiting for the killer to show herself and he needed a drink with friends.

The valets parked his Corvette and ushered him into the restaurant. It was early evening on a late summer night and customers were lining up waiting to be seated. When Reed came in and swung her around in a hug, Gina looked up in surprise and then smiled at one of her favorite friends.

"Why Reed Conners, you always manage to surprise me!" She exclaimed. "When did you come to town?"

"Just recently," he answered.

"Give me a few minutes and I'll join you inside."

When Reed walked into the bar, it was filled two and three deep with customers. When Paul saw him come in, a Crown Royal straight up was passed over the bar to him. Reed nodded his thanks, and savored the

"Nectar of the Gods," as he was prone to think of it at these times.

Coming in to join him, Paul had Gina's special bourbon on ice waiting for her. Tonight her shimmering blonde hair was done in a short and curly new look. Her frilly blue silk dress stopped just at the top of her knees and her legs were encased in nude colored hose. Her sling pumps were blue as well.

Reed looked her over. "God damn woman, if you don't get younger and better looking every time I see you!" He bent over and kissed her cheek.

"Ah ha, it shows then? My dear, it's this new pill and serum I'm taking, that I swear has reversed the calendar years by leaps and bounds!" Gina smiled into her bourbon as she took a hefty sip.

"Really? Are you at an acceptable age so you could marry me now?" Reed leaned over to her. "Or are you still too much of a woman for me?"

She laughed. "Sweetie, we'd probably have to kill each other if we got together." And their banter went on good-naturedly for a while.

"I met a mutual friend a few days ago. Daisy O'Dell? She stopped in for lunch," Gina said then.

Reed nodded. "She's had a bit of trouble and came here to regroup." Was all he wanted to divulge.

"A bit of trouble, for God's sake, she's in a lot more than that; She told me, a girlfriend is dead, someone is out to kill her, and poisonous snakes have driven her out of her home!"

Reed nodded, "And now we need to get the fucker!"

After finishing several Crown Royals, Reed stood up and brushed her cheek with another kiss. "Okay, my friend. Thanks for the drinks and I'll get back to you soon." He tipped the valets outside generously when they brought the Corvette around and he spun out into the street. Maybe he'd give it up for tonight and find that hotel. Goddamn, he'd been going since dawn.

But first too he needed to take a minute and connect with another special friend he'd been neglecting lately, and scrolled down on his cell to her number as he drove through the streets of Minneapolis. When Mona's smoky voice came over the line, she asked, "So where have you been keeping yourself?"

Attempting to answer nonchalantly he said, "I've been home at the lake and taking some time to relax."

And not being one to mince words, Mona asked, "I'll bet! Is that Lewis woman hanging around too?"

Reed laughed. "You know me so well, Mona. Yup, she's been hanging her hat there for a while again."

"Well, are you married yet?" She asked teasingly.

"Nah, but I want to know, how are you?"

"I feel wonderful Reed, my oncologist says I am in remission."

"Mona that's great. Can we get together sometime soon?"

Mona laughed, "I always get Lindy's leftovers. But that would be swell, Reed, and then I can tell you about my trip to Paris."

"So you went after all. Did your sister go with you?"

"Yes, she did. We had a grand time visiting the museums and seeing their magnificent art. The food was exquisite, of course."

"I'm sure. Did you fall in love or in lust?" And they both laughed.

"Of course," Mona quipped, "many times."

"Yah? Okay. Now beautiful, when do you want to get together?" He asked.

"Call me for when and where. Will that work?" Mona exclaimed.

"Yup, sure does." Reed answered.

-17-

Daisy suddenly tossed the book she had been reading across the room. She had been sitting drinking coffee and reading a latest novel, when her whole situation got the best of her. Despairingly, she raised her voice in a loud scream, but it was a pitiful replica of what was going on in her thoughts.

For God's sake, she couldn't even let loose here in her jail-like safe house, or someone would certainly call someone! But she just couldn't sit still here any longer. She swiped a hand over her suddenly tear covered face and ran to open the front door, determined to find a way back to familiar surroundings. However, when she turned the knob she found the door was locked, then sucking in her breath and running to the one leading out of the kitchen, she found that was locked as well.

"Oh- no," she cried out in the silence filled house. Why had they locked her in? She wasn't the enemy! She stumbled to a kitchen chair and sat down defeated. Then she remembered the cell phone she had bought awhile back and ran to find the coat pocket she had left it in. Raising that to her ear, she heard the dial tone. First of all she had to contact Ed, and let him know where she was. She found him at his house and when he answered, he yelled, "Where the hell, are you Daisy? I've called every hotel in that God forsaken town!"

"Ed. I'm sorry," Daisy apologized and her voice rose. "But that woman broke into my hotel room and now I'm locked in at a 'safe house.'" She went on to describe waking up to find the woman standing over her in her bed at the hotel. Where she ran and screamed out of the room.

"Oh Christ, Daisy," was all Ed could say for the moment. Then went on, "I finally reached Reed, but he didn't tell me much."

"What did he say?" Daisy asked curiously.

"Only that you were safe!"

"I am for now Ed, but, how you are?" Daisy needed to know. "I'm so sorry you got hurt in this mess."

"I know, but well, like they say, shit happens! But aside, I'm getting around on crutches and the pain is better. The doc says soon I can try walking with a cane."

"Oh God, I'm sorry." She repeated almost in pain too for him. "Ed, tell me, have you got someone there to help you?"

"I have, and I've been trying to convince her to give me a 'sponge bath.'" Ed chuckled then breaking the tension between them.

"Really? Is she good-looking?" Daisy joked feeling better.

"Oh yeah, and young." Ed went on.

"So I've got competition, then?" Daisy teased.

"Yup, so you better get back soon or I might run off with her!" Ed's chuckle was a little heartier.

"That so? Seriously Ed, I don't know when this will be over. But I promise I'll call you again in a day or two." After that, hanging up she went to turn on the television for the national news. And was aghast as a world-famous journalist started off with; "Tonight, we have breaking news that an assassin, a woman, who has been stalking a prominent Minnesota resident, is in custody. She is being held in a jail cell awaiting charges. The police department in Minneapolis, MN and the FBI are hopeful she is the last of a group of monstrous individuals who have been storming a small friendly town in the upper mid-west. We will have more on this as the story unfolds."

Daisy stood riveted to the television screen as she realized this story was about her. For God's sake, her thoughts began running amok, this mess had reached outlandish proportions, and now how soon would it be before her face and name would appear for the world to see. Chills spread over her shoulders as she looked around at her meager surroundings in the safe house. How long would she have to hide and stay locked up?

-18-

Reed Conners set the GPS in his Corvette to the address of The Franklin. A college buddy had recently opened a five star hotel located on the lakeshore of Minnetonka Bay. It had been several years since they had caught up with each other. And now, since Louie had lived in Europe for years, he might know something about the "guns for hire" business. Also, Reed needed a new address for himself while he was in Minneapolis.

Louie Liu and Reed got to be good buddies when they had shared an apartment in a run-down house on the campus of the U of M, where Louie had studied financial banking and Reed, the legal system. They'd drunk gallons of beer and burned the midnight oil, and raised hell with the women through their first three years of college. Then Reed had met Lindy Lewis and instantly cooled his jets and settled down to one. Louie had graduated with top honors and began to travel cutting a swat across Europe taking jobs in hotels and even dives to further his knowledge of management and sales in hostelry. That had catapulted into starting his first hotel and restaurant which led to numerous successful businesses in the UK.

It had been several years since Reed had connected with him, not since he had located Louie in Paris on one of his jaunts over there. Louie was of Scandinavian descent, with a little Korean thrown in which gave him a slim body and sexy eyes, which women loved, Reed remembered. He was always tanned and smart as hell. Several months ago Reed had read an article about his old friend opening another new restaurant of his own right here in the US in the twin cities of Minneapolis and Saint Paul, Minnesota.

The sun was going down as Reed drove out to Minnetonka and between his dark glasses and the Corvette's visor; he was still almost blinded as he spun along into the summer's golden glow. The traffic was stop and go, due to the road repairs and he forced himself to stay calm. City traffic always drove him to cussing flagrantly.

"Goddamnit," he cussed and banged his hand on the steering wheel. Where the hell was everybody going? Shouldn't they all be home sitting around a dinner table? "Ah hell," he mumbled, "I don't have to be anywhere soon, so relax!" And he stretched his legs out as he waited for the crunch of cars to get moving. He was anxious to see Louie.

The hotel was called The Franklin and as Reed swung off the freeway and up to the front he had a minute to glance at the landscaping. It was beautifully laid out with tiers of shrubs, flowers and tall trees, reminiscent of Roman gardens. The building itself was low, white with pillars across the huge front area. Outside dining was in full swing under gaily colored umbrella topped tables on one side of the building amongst the beautiful landscape next to the lake. Tuxedo clad waiters busily spun in amongst the customers delivering roast duck, fresh seafood flown in daily, and delicacies from continents across the map with price tags that could pay a working man's rent for a month.

Reed smiled as he took in his friend's new enterprise. The guy always had class and seeing the luxurious vehicles parked closely around the establishment, he was pleased to see what the traffic could bear. He went inside the restaurant to a bar and ordered Crown Royal over ice, his usual.

"Is Mr. Liu in this evening?" He asked the bartender.

"And may I give him your name sir?" The good looking woman behind the bar asked politely.

Reed grinned. "Tell him his buddy Conners from college."

"Hey, I've heard about you. You're the one who drove that babe bomb, the Corvette!" She laughed.

Reed looked her over more carefully. "I guess," he answered amused, but unsure where this was going.

She stepped closer, "Louie has regaled us over and over with stories of his college days with you in this town." She reached a hand over the bar and said, "My name is Vickie."

Reed extended his, not without first giving her a quick once over, and was pleasantly rewarded by seeing her stunning, eye popping beauty. She was tall, blond, bronzed and buffed, with long legs and long hair. She wore black short, shorts and a white tuxedo shirt, slightly open down almost to her waist. A sexy fragrance hovered over the bar and awakened Reed's senses to sudden lust.

"Wow," he said under his breath and ran a hand over his forehead, then brushed his hair back.

"Wait a sec and I'll page Mr. Liu for you," Vickie said and turned back to the bar and spoke on a cell.

Out of habit, Reed quickly put her age at late thirties or early forties, and her height and weight beautifully proportioned. He stepped back from the bar as if punched in his solar plexus. Goddamn, he mumbled at his own reaction and reached to the bar again for his Crown Royal and took a healthy drink of his whiskey.

Adding lightness to the moment he joked using that old adage, "Now where have you been all my life, beautiful lady?"

Vickie laughed again and kept the banter going. "Looking for you, handsome!"

"Well you've found me!" He swiped again at the fallen hair on his forehead. "Seriously, how long have you worked for Louie?" Reed asked then.

"I'm from London and I'd worked in his place over there for a few years. Then I had this opportunity to relocate here to the US."

"How do you like us so far?" Reed asked, noting a faint English accent.

Vickie smiled. "Well, I'm finding people drive too slow, eat too much and too many are overweight."

Reed laughed. "Yes, well, that about sums us up, I think." Just then Louie Liu walked in the bar.

"Conners, you never change, still trying to pick up the most beautiful ones, I see." And the two men exchanged man hugs.

"Louie, good to see you buddy." Reed stepped back and smiled at his friend.

"Same here, I've been looking for you to stop in." Louie remarked then.

"Sorry, I've been tied up with a case in Birch Lake, but it's moved down here now." Reed offered.

"Really? You need to fill me in. But first, I need to show you around. What do you think so far?" As Louie waved a hand around.

Reed noticed his hair was grayer now, but of course cut in a handsome style. He had his usual tailor-made look; this evening in a cream colored long sleeved silk shirt with chestnut brown linen slacks and shining brown Faragamo loafers, with no socks. The cuffs on his shirt were rolled up once to show a gold bracelet gleaming on one slim wrist and a Patek Philippe watch enhancing the other.

"Louie, I think each one you open just gets better and better! You have the know-how, my friend!" Reed offered.

"Well, I learn something new each time, believe me, and each time my hair gets grayer and I lose too much weight." Louie chewed his bottom lip.

Reed could see he was thinner. "Well, that's one way to keep it off. But I think what you need soon Louie is a visit to Birch. Then you can just lie back on my boat and count the stars, and I'll cook for you for a change."

"Amen to that. I figure in a month or two, I can leave the place to my GM to baby-sit for a few days and I'll be there. I remember the autumns there are breathless!"

"It's one of our best shows. I figure it starts the first week of October."

Louie nodded. "Then I'll plan on that. For now, let me show you around."

He led the way through the dining rooms, of which there were three. The third and biggest room was where elegance prevailed and no man was allowed in without a tie. And, you did not have to wear socks but you had to be wearing beautiful shoes. And in every area Louie showed him throughout The Franklin, Reed saw only well dressed, affluent people who were enjoying foods cooked by chefs from around the world.

Several months ago, on a special trip to Minneapolis and Nordstrom's to shop, Reed had invested in a new look. He had changed his entire wardrobe from jeans and sweaters to silk shirts and tailored slacks, baby soft leathers, both in jackets and boots. So tonight, his casual black shirt and slacks, and silver accessories, blended in perfectly with the rich and pampered clientele at The Franklin.

Lyn LaCoursiere

-19-

Ed Harrison tossed the covers off and maneuvered his hurting body out of the king sized bed. Jesus Christ, it was hell trying to just get out of it every day. Not only had he lost his canes somewhere on the floor overnight, but he had to have one for each leg! He groaned and the bedroom was blue with cussing as he slid his body near the edge and groped around for his legs, as he called them.

It seemed like a long time since the shooting had taken place at his business in Birch Lake, but actually only several weeks had gone by. Since then, the town had buried his good friend and valued employee who had been murdered by that maniac woman, and his other two men had been lucky to still have their lives. He had withstood hours of surgery on his busted knees that she had shot, but Christ, he was still alive. After making the mistake of bedding that crazy woman at one of his parties on his boat, he would think twice about letting strangers on board ever again.

He thought again of Daisy and the painful time she was going through after losing her close friend and her home to this deranged lot of psychopathic killers. In a way, he couldn't blame her for saying she was thinking of selling her house here in Birch and relocating again to the city.

But for Christ's sake, what about him? But what the hell could he do about it anyway. She really hadn't shown a great interest in him. Oh yeah, she let him watch over her for a while there, then she had just gotten in her car and driven away while he lay in the hospital trussed up like a Thanksgiving turkey, out of his head with pain.

Christ, he was tired of it all. Tired of the doctors and the hurt; both in his body and also in his heart. He was limping down the hallway when his doorbell chimed. It took him many minutes to finally get to the front door and when he opened it, Lindy Lewis stood there.

"Hello, Ed, can I come in?" She asked, looking suntanned and trim in white shorts and a yellow t-shirt.

Too surprised to say anything, Ed stood leaning on his canes in his pj's. His morning hair was tousled.

"Yes, please," he said and carefully maneuvered to the side of the doorway.

"I know this is a surprise Ed, but you see I've decided to leave Reed's house and go away. And I just needed someone to say goodbye to." She looked downcast as she stood there.

"Well, come in and have a cup of coffee with me before you leave, Lindy." Actually Ed was glad to have company. He was not used to being laid up alone at home. And Christ, he was lonesome!

"Are you sure it's okay?" Lindy asked again. "I drove through town one last time, and you were the only one I wanted to say goodbye to. You were always nice to me, Eddy."

"Well, Reed is my friend. Why wouldn't I be? Come on in Lindy, I haven't been to the kitchen yet to start any."

"Okay," she said following him slowly as he made his way. Coming into the streamlined gourmet room, she motioned him to a chair. "Let me start the coffee and you sit and take it easy. Just tell me where and how to find everything," she said taking charge.

Ed sank down in relief. He had a full time housekeeper but she didn't come in until later, and his nurse's aide didn't come in until evening to check over his progress. The last few days, he had been getting by on his own, but he was tired of it all. And glad of this sudden turn of events.

"Where is Reed?" He asked Lindy now as she bustled around his kitchen.

She turned to him. "He's off again on one of his jaunts, this time he's in Minneapolis saving the world," she murmured and a bit of sarcasm edged her remark.

Careful not to read a wrong message, he asked, "So, does Reed know that you're leaving, and how does he feel about it?"

Lindy carefully plugged in the coffee pot and came over and took a chair. "Eddy, let me speak frankly. I've come to the realization that we don't mean much to each other. I come back here when I need help, and he takes me in out of habit, and it's time for a change, for me as well as him!" She swiped at a tear.

Immediately Ed had a thought, albeit a crazy one, for Christ's sake. But he cleared his throat, but really what the hell could he say, Reed was his friend!

-20-

Daisy O'Dell suddenly awoke out of a sound sleep and stumbled out of bed and ran to the bathroom and hung her head in the commode. For long minutes, her life was suspended in hell as she gasped and choked in the darkened room. She was already on her knees around the toilet bowl and now weakened, she sagged to the floor and lay. She didn't know how long she had lain there, but she awoke again as chills from the cold floor tiles shuddered through her body. A sliver of a harvest moon lit up the small room from around the sides of a shade at a small window up high on a wall. She pulled herself up to the sink and turned the cold water on and splashed her face and rinsed her mouth, all the while hanging on to the edge of the counter for balance with one hand. Then, taking small careful steps and leaning against the walls, she managed to get back to the safety of her bed, but the room tumbled and spun around her. She grabbed on to the blankets, but that didn't anchor the kaleidoscope of colors and objects from dancing in and out of her sight.

She was terribly sick, but who could help her? Reed or that nice cop called Murphy? Maybe she could call Billy Miller! Her thoughts were random and mixed. Should she call 911 for the paramedics, but then what was the address here in this "safe house." Just where the hell was she? Oh, God, she didn't remember, somewhere in Minneapolis. Then it was all too much and Daisy closed her eyes and prayed for sleep, wiping away helpless tears. And then, blissfully, slumber did finally spread throughout her weary body, and she slept again.

-1- 25

Reed spent his next night in the comforts of the Franklin Hotel, which his friend Louie Liu owned in Minneapolis. This morning, as he lay awake he thought over the conversation they had had the night before.

As they sat in the privacy of a booth, Reed asked, "Louie, I need to know what you can tell me about the underworld of guns for hire that originate in Europe."

Louie sat back in the leather padded booth and ran a hand over his trimmed mustache. He was silent with a thoughtful look on his face.

Reed went on, "I'm sure you've read in the papers about the upheaval my town is going through again."

"Sure." Louie took a drink of his McAllen's Bourbon.

"Then you're aware of what we are up against. We have had three deaths so far and another assassin has followed us here to Minneapolis." Reed said.

"My friend, what I'm not sure of is what the hell is going on Reed?" Louie raised his shoulders as he questioned.

"Let me start at the beginning Louie, it goes back to several months ago, when one of the Birch Lakes residents was expecting a visit from her friend who lived in Oslo, Norway." He went on to explain that the man she had been sleeping with was a hired killer. And, that when she threatened to leave, he declared he 'would kill her, if she tried'. Well, she tried and he did, then he died and his accomplices took over. We got three so far, and now we have a fourth, a woman." Reed finished and took a big swallow of his Crown Royal and wished he had a cigarette.

"Jesus, man, this sounds like something out of a movie script." Louie stared at Reed. "If you got the belly of the underworld stirred up you'll have a hard time putting an end to it."

"That's what I know. We've killed three of their operatives so far. But listen to this, now we've got this one behind bars."

"Damn!" Louie exclaimed.

"We got her yesterday, so she's downtown cooling her heels in a cell." Reed hunched his shoulders to relieve some tension.

"Okay, that could be good, Reed." Louie ran his hands over his face, slowly as though massaging it. He was silent. Then he said, "My friend, you'll never get rid of them. Jesus, as long as you keep killing their people, they'll keep sending more to even the score."

"That's what I'm afraid of." Reed sat back then but drummed his fingers on the table top. "Louie, what do you think of trying to make a deal with them?" He asked then.

Louie was silent. "It might work since you have one of them." He said nodding his head, and then went on, "I might know some people, let me make some calls. What could you offer them?" Louie asked.

Without hesitation Reed declared. "We'll give her back to them, alive, for a guaranteed end of this reign of terror!"

Reed had never pried into Louie's life, but he figured Louie carried a lot of weight in the UK, just by what he'd surmised the times he had visited his friend over there.

Louie stood up. "Reed, give me two hours and I'll get back to you."

"Okay buddy, I appreciate it. You can reach me on my cell." And Reed went to his room to catch up on some sleep.

Lyn LaCoursiere

-21-

The next morning Daisy awakened to the strange and silent house and looked around for something familiar. It was all foreign to her again, until she saw the shuttered window in the bedroom and then remembered she was in what was called a "safe house". A safe house, for God's sake, it was a damned prison! It didn't look like anyone could get in, and she wasn't sure if she could even get out.

She tossed the washed out covers off and stood up, then felt the weakness in her body and remembered the awful time she had spent in the bathroom during the night. This had happened before and how sick she had been then too, but whatever it was, today she felt okay. She hadn't had a chance to take anything with her to this place, so all she had were the clothes on her back and very little make-up, as everything was still at the last hotel she'd had to vacate. The people who brought her here had said, there were enough essentials to get by on, 'you won't be here long.' Already another night had been too long.

Daisy ran her hands through her blonde hair restlessly. What the hell would she do another day here? She reached for her cell phone. At least she had that with her, but what good was it? She couldn't call her best friend as she was dead. Yes, Roma was dead, she said out loud shaking her head. It was hard to believe even now, weeks later. For a moment, Daisy felt tears threaten again and she swiped at them. She just couldn't cry again. God, it seemed she'd feel totally cried out, until the tears would come over her again and she'd lose it, again. She put on the faded robe that had hung in the closet and tied it around her waist and went to the kitchen. There was coffee in the cupboard, and some food in the refrigerator; TV dinners and breakfast dishes but no fresh fruits or vegetables.

She turned on the television for company and stopped dead in her tracks when this time she saw a TV announcer actually standing by her house in Birch Lake. She said, "And here folks, is where it all started. This is where she lived, but of course has now disappeared. I ask you now, is Daisy O'Dell innocent or is she a murderer?"

Well, Daisy just stood there and gawked at the screen, for a minute unable to comprehend what the story had elevated to. Then it dawned on her, that now the media had turned it around to put the blame on her. Not that she had been forced to shoot in self-defense when Gunther Mueller found her in Ed's house. When the sociopath had broken in and was seconds away from strangling her with that noose around her neck.

Daisy put her hands in her hair and messaged her sore head, then rushed over to the TV and checked the other channels. She found a normal morning show and got her coffee and sat down to watch whatever they had to offer.

She tried to calm down as the day wore on. And after doing what she could without much make-up, except for the old jar of Pond's cold cream she'd found in the bathroom to moisturize with, she called it good. For God's sake, who would see her anyway?

Later in the day when her cell phone rang, she clutched it in relief, then heard attorney, Billy Miller on the line.

"Daisy, I'm just checking to see if you are okay."

"Outside of hearing I'm considered a murderer now, you mean?"

"Where did you hear that?" He asked.

Daisy gripped the cell. "I heard it on channel six around nine o'clock this morning."

"Jesus, those people should be fired. Listen, do I have your permission to call there and threaten a law suit, if it is repeated again?" He asked.

"Oh lord, Bill, absolutely! And, that goes to anybody else who dares to mention the word. I've had it!"

"Do you want me to come over?" He asked then.

Daisy was silent for a minute. God, she was lonely, and he was a perfect lover. But for some reason her thoughts went back home to Ed Harrison. Now that she was totally alone and things were deadly quiet, she'd had time to think more clearly. And she recalled that hitch in his voice when she'd said she was not coming back to Birch and they'd said goodbye. She thought over the times she'd stayed at his house and he'd put his life on the line for her, and he had more than once.

"Bill," she said then. "Thanks, but no. I'll check with you in a day or two."

"If you're sure, Daisy. Listen, the thirty day waiting period in your case is soon up from the opposing team, namely the Hurst boys. I haven't even heard a rumble around the halls of justice about this case. It could be they won't contest the issue."

"Well, I've got mixed emotions about all of it. And Bill, I don't have any idea of what Roma's assets consists off." She chewed on a nail, as she talked.

"Daisy, this will surprise you then, as far as I can tell, we're talking approximately ten million!" Daisy dropped the coffee cup in her lap and jumped up. "Good God almighty, millions?" She gasped.

"Yes, Daisy. We are talking about millions."

Daisy frantically brushed at the hot coffee with one hand as it seeped through the faded leopard print of the robe and burned her skin.

"But I can't, I thought maybe around a hundred thousand. But millions? No-!"

"It's true. There's that bank in the Caymans. You can't get in the door with less than five mil. From what I've been able to find so far, I'd say easily ten."

Daisy tossed the coffee soaked robe off and now sat without a stitch on. Then she clicked off the cell and smiled, and began to laugh and dance around the room. She didn't care if anyone heard her. She just laughed, hysterically until those damn tears came again.

Lyn LaCoursiere

-22-

Reed had been dosing in the easy chair in his room at The Franklin, Louie Liu's hotel, when his cell phone awakened him.

"Reed, this is Louie." He heard.

Immediately Reed woke up. "Hello." he said to his friend. He had been waiting as Louie had offered to make some calls to the UK to some people he knew who might be helpful in the negotiations for an end to this reign of terror on his town and Daisy O'Dell's life.

"I made a few calls and here's what they say." Louie went on. "They want the prisoner back, but they won't guarantee an end to this war, as they call it."

Reed was ready. "No dice. Tell them she's charged with attempted murder and she'll be found guilty and get the chair."

"Really they don't care about saving the prisoner's life, just that she will sing like a bird in order to make a deal."

"Louie, tell them she looks ready to sing now. Tell them we will give them another two hours. If we don't get a guarantee of peace then, negotiations are over!" Reed lit up a cigarette and blew a smoke ring toward the ceiling as he talked.

"Alright, I will relay your thoughts. Reed, my friend, I'm sorry you are troubled."

"Thanks Louie, I'm okay. And I appreciate all you can help us with buddy. I'll wait for your reply."

And Reed clicked off the cell. Now he was wide awake, and he turned on the wide screen television and settled in to catch the news of the day and sat up as he saw the recap of the morning broadcast and a picture of a familiar house in Birch Lake.

And, when the commentator asked, 'Is Daisy O'Dell a murderer?' he swore.

'Goddamn it,' no wonder the media gets beaten up! He dialed Murphy's cell, it was after 10'clock at night.

Anne Murphy answered and exclaimed, "It's so good to hear your voice, Reed! When can you come over? The girls and I would love to see you."

It wasn't so long ago that Reed had found Ann's almost lifeless body in the Grain Belt Building after being kidnapped by that psycho called Wolff. Reed was also Godfather to her two girls.

"Thanks Anne," he said, "Hopefully in a day or two we'll have this case put to bed."

"I'm counting on it. Here's John." Murphy picked up saying, "What's up?"

Reed went on. "Louie heard from them and so far it's no dice. They'll take the prisoner back but won't promise peace."

"Fuckers," Murphy exhaled into the receiver.

"Murph, I told Louie to tell them, no deal! And that she's ready to talk." Reed leaned back in the soft chair as he talked. "I said to tell them we'll give them another two hours. And if they don't agree then, we're prepared to pin every known charge there is against her to keep her behind bars. And, we'll get every piece of info she knows about anyone out of her as she tries to save her ass."

"That'll make them nervous. Reed, what do you think, if this gets them off our ass, will they really lay off?"

"Here's what I thought we should do, Murph. See what you think. It's a double cross. We sweat her until we've wrung every bit of goods out of her. But, we tell them she told us a "few" things, then clammed up. But that we will move on this info if we even think, their people have come back to the US."

"Yeah, that might work. And if she has any smarts at all, she'll get to another part of the world if she wants to keep her ass alive." Reed kicked off his boots and stretched out his legs on an ottoman.

"Okay, I'll wait to hear then after Liu connects with you." And they disconnected.

It was now going on midnight and Reed settled into waiting the several hours for the next call. He didn't want to fall asleep but wanted to stay alert until he heard back from Louie. He turned the sound down on the television and put his head back and closed his eyes. His thoughts were still churning around in his head until they settled on a niggling one that had been edging its way up for attention.

Goddamn, he muttered now, feeling irritated at the intrusion. He didn't have time now for this. Intuitively he knew it involved Lindy Lewis. He dialed his telephone in the house in Birch Lake, and got no answer. But looking at the time, however, he reasoned by now she would be in bed sound asleep. He would check in tomorrow.

The two hours dragged on slowly but finally the call from Louie came through.

"Louie," Reed exclaimed into his cell. "Got some news?"

"They will take the prisoner back, but she's good as dead if she has leaked one iota of info about anything!" Louie went on.

"Of course, she's not going to come clean with them and admit she blew them off. Okay, how soon?" Reed exhaled.

"They said pack her up and send her back now." Louie commented dryly.

"What will they give us as a guarantee of their good faith?" Reed asked.

"They said we will have their trust and they, in turn, will trust the US to do the right thing now." Louie said tongue in cheek.

"Yeah right." Reed scoffed. "Well, okay. We'll start the process to get her out of here and on her way. Thanks buddy, for all your help."

"You're welcome Reed, happy to have helped. Stop in the office and let me know how things go."

And Reed immediately called Murph.

"Here's the deal," he said. "They want her back now, but if she talked she's dead. They guarantee their trust as they trust us."

"Yeah? And I believe in fairies." Murphy commented dryly. "That gives us just a couple of hours until the orders come through and are processed. Meet me in ten minutes, and I'll call MacGreger on the way." And they clicked off their cells.

It was going on three AM in the morning and in minutes Ursula Arickson would come, face to face with her three, most feared tormentors.

Lyn LaCoursiere

-23-

All Daisy had ever wanted years ago when she left Minneapolis was to have a peaceful life back in her home town of Birch Lake. She had been happy for years as she had her house built and started her own business and then settled in. But the last year had been nothing but hell now, after being sick in the middle of the night, again. Was it all the stress going on lately that was affecting her both emotionally and physically, or was it something else happening with her body?

She clicked off her cell after talking to attorney, Billy Miller, who had told her that he expected her case could be valued in the neighborhood of ten million dollars. She was still in shock.

Lyn LaCoursiere

For God's sake, it was unbelievable. She knew Roma Hurst had collected quite a handsome sum of money when she divorced her husband, but she had never mentioned the amount. Now all Roma Hurst's assets could come to her. Millions! But would Reed and his guys catch that freak who was trying to kill her in time? Or would she die too?

However, she dared to dream again. If those millions came to her, the first thing she would do would be to pay off her kid's loans and mortgages, and give them some money to play with. Then she would do what she and Roma had talked about years ago, and that was to buy that dance hall that stood on the shores of a nearby body of water called Maple Lake. It was old and rundown now, but still in operation with entertainment from all over the country. It was owned by an old man who lived in the town called Maple, twenty miles down the road from Birch Lake. Daisy had heard it was slated for closing soon, because it needed renovations and the owner didn't want to do them. He was getting too old and he didn't have any family. If, and there was a big if, all these millions came through, and they could get the place reasonably cheap, she would follow the dream she and Roma had of owning that dance hall. Only now, Roma was dead.

She found another robe in the closet and slipped it on, a man's flannel plaid this time. She sat down again and let her thoughts ramble. Wouldn't it be great to rebuild the old dance hall and use it for all sorts of occasions as well? There were huge potentials such as weddings, dinners, holiday parties, car and craft shows, and numerous classes of sorts. There was no end to the events that needed an up-scale establishment to show their wares.

Daisy's pen flew as she jotted down the possibilities of creating this venue for her dream business. She sketched the outside of the place from memory, and then the inside as she remembered. She hadn't been so excited for a long time. After the anguish of losing her best friend, and then having to leave her home and her manicuring business, she had been in a terrible place of depression and helplessness. Now maybe life would be good again for her.

She thought back to when she and Roma would daydream about being glamorous ladies who owned a club. How they would dress and how they would never get involved with their clientele. Daisy smiled when she remembered they couldn't decide if they would leave their husbands, or if they might be dead. Then Roma's had just been starting out as an inventor of medical devices and spent all his time in their basement tinkering and hers had been an up and coming doctor of cardiology. Both husbands had become successful in their careers and left their hard working wives alone to raise the kids, who had given up their own careers to help further theirs. Daisy remembered how hard she had worked to get over her hurt and anger about losing those years, and how good she had felt when she thought she had.

And now, for God's sake, maybe she could feel good again, and soon!

Her cell had rung then and it was Reed who said, "Daisy, I have just a minute but I wanted you to know, we got the stalker and she's behind bars."

Daisy clutched the robe around herself as chills slid down her back. "Really? At last!" She exclaimed.

"Just hang in there," he assured her.

"One minute, Reed, how can we be sure a new killer won't show up again?" Daisy asked.

"Daisy, you're safe now!"

"But, how do I know that another person won't show up?" Daisy persisted, almost in tears of frustration.

"We're working that out, Daisy," Reed tried to console her. "Listen, I'll get back to you in a few hours." He clicked off, understanding her anxiety.

Determined not to slip into a deep depression again, Daisy showered and washed and dried her one set of clothes. And using the meager supply of make-up she had along, she applied it and looked and felt better. Picking up her sheets of plans for the renovation of Maple Lake, she sat at the shabby table in the safe house kitchen and sketched late into the night. She looked at the clock and by now she thought that Reed and his friends must have left the jail. She wondered what the stalker had confessed to. Songs from the 80's played on the small plastic radio that sat on the cupboard and the ashtray at her side was full of cigarette butts. Soon hunger pangs sent her to the refrigerator in search of something for a late snack. And piling cheese and turkey on a slice of grain bread, she added a glass of milk, and settled in again to dream and plan into the wee hours. Finally, tossing the robe on a wooden chair in the bedroom, Daisy opened the faded chenille bedspread on the bed and fell into it, dog-tired, but only tossed and turned. Not knowing that at this very moment, just before the sun came up over the city, Reed, Murphy and FBI Agent McGreger were still intensely interviewing Ursela Arickson downtown at the jail.

Lyn LaCoursiere

-24-

Reed threw on his clothes and hastily brushed his teeth and was out the door of his hotel room in a couple of minutes. At three in the morning, the traffic was sparse and he careened down the parking ramp and over the few blocks to the court house where the jail was located. Taking the elevator down a floor, he took a seat in a waiting area to watch for Murph and MacGreger. Looking around he found just what he needed and took out a couple of single bills to put in a coffee machine. It wasn't Starbucks but it was hot and strong, and just what he needed. After several minutes, both Murphy and MacGreger came in and Murphy went to the glassed in area and pushed a buzzer. After putting his ID up to a window, and explaining the situation all three were finally let in and then told to go to room A to wait for the prisoner.

Ten minutes, then fifteen went by as they sat silently and waited.

"Goddamn, are they purposely stalling?" Reed asked breaking the silence.

"Nah," Murph said. "It takes time for the message to be handed over. Then she might be pissed at being awakened and refuse to come out, and if she finds out it's us again, she might dig her heels in and they'll have to drag her in here."

"Is this room wired?" Reed asked then.

"No." Murphy exclaimed. "Against the law, you know."

FBI agent MacGreger smiled at that. "Well, it depends on where you are." He said then. "Some are and some aren't." He opened the brown suede jacket he had on and took out a pipe and absently puffed on the cold fumes.

Just then, the door opened and the prisoner stood there. "Not you again," she yelled and tried to back out of the room, but the door had closed behind her.

"Yeah, it's us again Arickson. And we're not leaving. So you might as well come in and take a seat." Reed said and rolled up his shirtsleeves as the room suddenly seemed warm.

They knew Ursula Arickson was thirty nine years old, five four and a hundred and thirty pounds. Born in Oslo, Norway, and there, the history stopped. It was all they had on her until she had been taken into custody here in the US.

She turned around to the door and began to pound on it and yelled, "Open up, get me out of here." And when no one came, she pounded and yelled louder. This went on for a while and the heat in the room slowly crept up a few more degrees.

MacGreger took his jacket off. Murphy threw his sweat shirt on the table.

Ursula was a natural born blonde with a short boy haircut, and icy blue eyes. Her complexion was pale and her body, muscular. A scar ran through her upper lip and into her left cheek, sometimes making her speech sound like she was lisping. She was a good looking woman and stood defiantly in her orange jumpsuit as she banged fruitlessly on the door with her hands. Reed just sat relaxed and watched the theatrics.

None of the guys said anything and just watched as the woman starting cussing, using words they even shook their heads at hearing. This went on for a good thirty minutes and finally Murphy stood and said, "Okay, Miss Arickson, you can yell and bang on that door till your blue in the face, but they have our orders not to open it unless we say so. So you decide, do you want to talk to us now, or later?"

Reed reached in a paper bag and handed her a bottle of water which she took and drank from greedily. And the heat went up another few degrees and McGreger took off his sweater vest.

"What do you want from me? You can't force me to talk to you!" she whispered, hoarsely. Sweat began to run down her forehead and trail over her cheeks. "You fuckers! Make me!"

"Ursula come and sit down. Why don't you tell us about yourself," Reed asked.

MacGreger stepped close to where she sat at the table. "What we need are some names, Miss Arickson." He grabbed the next chair and put his face right in her space.

"Hey, get away from me," she growled. The heat rushed out of a vent located right over her seat at the table. She stood up abruptly, "Jesus Christ, why the hell is it so fucking hot in here?'

"Hot, it's not hot in here. I'm comfortable. Aren't you guys?" Murphy commented looking innocently at Reed and MacGreger. Unbeknownst to her, they were taking turns stepping over to and under a cold air vent in the corner of the small room.

"Let me out of here. What names? I don't know what you're talking about." She yelled still standing and defiantly glaring at them.

Murphy watched as sweat trickled down her face. "Sit down, Ursula, you might as well know your country won't take you back, so you're going to have to find a new one." Then nodding at MacGreger he said, "This here is Federal agent MacGreger. That's the FBI, you know. I'll let him tell you this."

MacGreger took his time putting his cold pipe that he still held, back in his shirt pocket.

"Now here's the deal, give us the names of your associates and maybe, just maybe if we believe you, we'll let you loose to look for that new country that you'll need to go to."

"I know your tactics. You're all a fucking bunch of liars!" She spit out.

Reed stepped in and handed her another bottle of water. She took the second and gulped it down. And in his calm voice said, "Miss Arickson, we don't care where you go, and in fact, we don't want to know. Once you've given us what we want to know. I'll personally walk you to the door."

"Ya, right, and how can you protect me? If I talk I'm dead." She growled.

They were all quiet. Purposely.

"Jesus Christ, let me out, I need to go to the bathroom!" She suddenly exclaimed.

"Hmm-," Murphy looked off in the distance. Reed and MacGreger didn't hear her. The men didn't move or acknowledge her plea.

"Can't you understand, I need to use the bathroom, didn't you hear me?" Her voice rose.

"Sorry," Murphy shook his head and his shoulders.

"What the hell, I need to go now!" She jumped up and ran to the door and started banging on it again.

The guys still just sat there and calmly looked at her. Time went by.

"Can't you understand?" Ursula yelled and banged. Twenty some minutes went by then, as she stood defiantly with her back to them and her lips in a thin line. Then she screamed again, "I need to go now. Now!" She turned around and faced them and just then looked down at herself in horror, and they all watched in silence as a wet spot appeared on the front of her orange suit and spread slowly down her pant legs.

"Oh no—"she cried then. "I peed in my pants. Look what you fuckers made me do." She glared at them and turned and pounded again on the door.

"Now you know we are not letting you out, Miss Arickson." MacGreger said. "Sorry, you will have to sit in your own mess, and you may as well sit down now and start talking. The sooner you do, the sooner you can get out of here."

They had been in the room for almost three hours and the heat in the room had gone up to 90 degrees, and now the smell of urine mixed with the odor of her fear. Her face was red and blotchy and sweaty, and her blond hair looked as if she had just come in out of the rain.

"Fuckers, fuckers," she spit out again. And she looked down at herself then flung her arms up in the air. "Look what you made me do!" For just a second, she looked like she was going to tear up, but then it passed and her face tightened again in rage, as she whispered now.

"What the fuck do you want to know, assholes?"

"Names of your buddies, Miss Arickson!" Reed exclaimed.

"Fuckers," she growled. MacGreger reached in a pocket and took out his tape recorder and calmly placed it on the table right in front of her. The three men gathered close as dawn began its accent into the city, hopefully, they would soon get out of the hell-hole to the fresh air outside.

Lyn LaCoursiere

-25-

Daisy tossed and turned until around six in the morning then finally threw the blankets off and got up out of the bed.

"For God's sake," she said disgustingly, out loud to the empty house, "Why am I not at home sleeping on my own thousand dollar mattress? Instead of in this flop house somewhere here in Minneapolis. And I don't even know where," she added as she put on the faded men's bathrobe again. In the kitchen she found the coffee and started a fresh pot, then turned on the television. Without listening to a news man tell of the happenings in the city overnight, she went into the bathroom and turned on the shower.

Lyn LaCoursiere

Today, after not getting a good night's sleep, her body ached and hurt all over. So she stood and let the hot water sluice over herself and finally felt the pain and stiffness leave. Tying a towel around her chest, she opened the door and left it ajar to let the steam filled room air out and went back out to the kitchen for her coffee. It smelled heavenly out there and she filled a cup, then turned to face the TV as an announcer's voice caught her attention when he said, "she died instantly!"

Daisy froze and she grabbed at the towel as it began to slide down over her hips.

Something told her this involved her? But who, what? Who was the announcer talking about? Then he went on to say, "This is all we know folks." And, went on to news from around the world.

Daisy tried other channels but couldn't find anything more. She tried Reed's cell, but it rang and rang and he didn't answer. Then she hurried to the bedroom and threw on her same clothes and went out again to the TV to listen. Nothing!

"For God's sake," she yelled. What the hell is going on? Were they talking about the stalker? The woman, the killer who was in jail downtown?

Daisy hurried into the bathroom again and gelled her hair, and fluffed it the best she could, then applied her make-up. But why hurry? She couldn't go anywhere. And she didn't know for sure who the TV announcer was talking about. He could have been telling about someone else here in the city. After all, it was a huge town with millions of people.

She paced around the apartment, drinking coffee and chain smoking as the hours went by. And finally the noontime news was announced. Daisy turned the sound up and took a seat on the couch and nervously chewed on a fingernail. Then a good looking newsman came on and said, "Here we are folks, in front of the police station in downtown Minneapolis where early this morning a woman prisoner stole a gun right out of a cop's holster and pointed it at her forehead and shot herself. She died instantly. As yet folks, we don't know her identity, but I'm told she may be from another country."

Daisy jumped up and grabbed her cell and tried Reed again, but he wasn't picking up. Beside herself with emotion she called Ed Harrison.

"Eddy," she said when he answered. "Listen, I think this horror story is coming to an end. Have you got the news on?" She babbled almost out of control.

"Daisy Mae," Ed said, "Where are you and what the hell do you mean. They caught that weirdo?"

Daisy took a breath. "Yes, at least I think so, and it says she shot herself. I can't get Reed on his cell."

"When did you last talk to him?" Ed asked.

"Last night and he said him and Murphy and MacGreger were all going down to the jail to see the stalker. And I haven't heard from him since."

"Jesus, let me turn on the TV and I'll call you back in ten minutes, Daisy." And they clicked off their cell phones.

Daisy hurried to the kitchen and put on another pot of coffee, then ripped open a new pack of Marlboros, guiltily thinking, maybe I'll get off these soon now!

When her cell rang she had been clutching it in her hand, waiting for Ed's call.

"Okay," he said, "what they're saying is a prisoner is dead, after stealing a cop's gun and turning it on herself. No mention of who it is, or who else it involves."

"I know, but it's them, Ed. It's got to be." Daisy hugged the cell with her shoulder as she poured some fresh coffee in her cup.

"I think you're right, Daisy. But until someone calls to verify that to you, you can't be totally sure." Ed said worriedly. "Christ, I wish I was there with you."

"Eddy, I'm sorry, I haven't asked how you're doing today." Daisy whispered.

"Hey, sweetie, I'm walking. Maybe pretty slow, but I'm on my own two feet!"

Daisy could hear him huff out a breath, as he must have sat down.

"You are? Oh Ed, I'm so relieved." Daisy said.

"Hey, I'm doing just fine. I just need to see the physical therapy doc for a few weeks yet."

"How is your auto business doing without you there?" She asked.

"It's just fine. I put my salesmen in charge until I can go back full time. I've just been going in part-time now."

"Wow, you heal fast. I still am so sorry you have to go through all this, Ed."

"Daisy Mae, it's not your fault that this happened," Ed replied. "I'll be good as new shortly, the doc says."

"Oh Lord, I can only hope. You know, if this is the end to this horror filled time, we all will need time to re-acess our options."

"Hmm-, what do you mean, Daisy?" Ed asked.

"Well, I have my beautiful home there in Birch and also my business that I worked so hard at getting it up and off the ground."

"I know. Your life is here, Daisy."

"I just need to take it slow, Eddie. My friend is doing a good job keeping my store open there. Thank God!"

"For sure." Ed Harrison commented.

"Okay. I'll call you when I hear something. Keep your TV on." And Daisy clicked off her cell and began to wait.

Lyn LaCoursiere

-26-

Murphy had jerked away from the prisoners lightening quick action as she had lunged at him. He had time to go for his gun, but in an instant she grabbed it right out of his hand, tried to point it at him and failing, turned it on herself. The three men stood immobilized in shocked silence as the gun shot echoed through the small interrogation room at the downtown police station. And Ursula Arickson had fallen to the floor, dead even before she hit it. Her blood and brains everywhere.

"Jesus," Murphy yelled as he had attempted to grab her.

"Goddammit," Reed exclaimed, and had jumped in and shoved Murphy out of the way just in time as she had attempted to take him out with his own gun.

"Watch out! Get her!" MacGreger had shouted just as the melee started.

It all took only about ten seconds and then it was over. Reed looked down at his shirt and swore, then almost lost it when he saw his trousers and shoes were covered with blood and gray matter. Murphy and MacGreger didn't look much better.

The door into the room flew open as more cops rushed in; their own guns drawn and ready.

"What the hell?" the first one shouted.

"Hold on," Murphy yelled to his mates. "She got my gun and took herself out. Get the chief!"

And within minutes the place quieted down as the burly chief ran in exclaiming, "Jesus Christ, Murphy, I heard and I need you three in my office now!" And after looking at the dead assassin lying on the floor in her own blood, he yelled and pointed, "Bag the gun, then her hands. The rest of you go on with your business. In the mean time someone get the ME."

"I need to find a restroom and clean up first," Reed mumbled under his breath. And went off down a hallway with MacGreger following. Murphy had walked out with his boss, the chief.

"Goddammit," Reed said as he grabbed a bunch of paper towels in there and began wiping off his clothes, then his expensive shoes. "How the hell could she get at his gun that fast?"

"She's a hired gun, remember? She would be fast and tricky." MacGreger turned on a faucet and ran water over his hands and then splashed his face. "Speed is what they're good at. But the film will show how it all came down." He said bending over the sink.

It was mid- morning and Reed, Murphy and MacGreger didn't leave the precinct until late afternoon, not until the chief was satisfied with their report. However, Murphy was put on unpaid leave awaiting a hearing with the IA, about his not being in control of his firearm at all times.

MacGreger needed to check in with the Minneapolis FBI people and Reed had things to do. But first he had to go by his hotel and get clean clothes. On the way he called Daisy.

"Daisy, sorry it took so long to get back to you," he said as he sped down a parking ramp. "I guess by now you must have heard on the TV what has gone on."

"Yes, I heard, but no names have been given out. Was it her?" Daisy whispered.

"Yep, it was her. She's gone."

"Oh Lord." The line was silent for a few moments as she shook her head. "I'm sorry a person died, but I'm not sorry it was her, Reed."

"You don't have to explain to me Daisy. Listen, I need to stop and change my clothes and then I'll come and get you."

"Oh God, I can't think straight right now Reed, but I'll be ready!" And Daisy tossed her cell on the bed. "Well, I've got nothing to pack, so I'm ready right now," she said to the walls and began to pace.

Reed also called Sheriff Jesse back home in Birch Lake. "Hey Jesse, guess you must have heard by now too." He said as he cruised through downtown Minneapolis, the Corvette humming beautifully.

"God almighty Conners, how in the hell did she get Murphy's gun. He's always so tight-fisted with it."

"That broad was quick, man. She tried to take him out, but when she missed her chance, she just raised it to her own head and pulled the trigger." Reed lit a cigarette while he waited at a stop sign to enter traffic.

"I guess by then she knew what lay ahead for her." The sheriff remarked. "How's Daisy?" he asked then.

"She's okay, thank God. She's been in a safe house for a few days however."

"Tell her to stop in when she gets back. Got to take off now."

"Listen, I'll be back in Birch by evening so I'll track you down." And Reed clicked off and tossed his cell on the seat of the Corvette.

-27-

Daisy smoked and paced and watched the clock. Several hours went by, and by late afternoon she was 'fit to be tied' as the expression goes. All she needed was for Reed to make the arrangements to get her out of the safe house program and she could be on her way.

She would go back to the hotel and get her possessions and her car. But she had worried, did she really want to stay here in the city after all, or go back to Birch Lake?

She was lonely. It had been nice to spend the evening with her attorney, Billy Miller. But she didn't see any future with him as she read him as a player; a very talented, smart attorney, but not one to get personally hung up on.

Hell, she was lonely for everything; her home, her business and her friends in Birch, and even for Romeo, her snake hunting dog which she'd sent back home with Reed weeks ago to bring back to the kennels. And, what about Ed Harrison? She missed him.

When the doorbell finally rang, she ran to open the door for Reed. And when he stepped in, she grabbed him and hugged him.

"Oh my God, Reed," she cried with relief, "It's finally over!"

"Just grab your purse and we're out of here," he said smiling.

She already had it ready by the door and in minutes they roared out of there.

The busy streets with the late afternoon traffic in Minneapolis, was a welcome sight again for Daisy and they arrived at the hotel where she had been staying prior to when the stalker had found her. It didn't take long for her to claim her suitcases, and locate her Porsche in the locked parking lot. She hugged Reed again.

"Are you anxious to get back to Birch?" He asked.

Daisy was silent for a minute. "I am. However I'm not too sure of things though."

"Okay, my friend, but don't do anything rash." He smiled and got in his car. "Follow me and drive carefully."

Then she was alone. Alone to think, and alone to drive the three hours back home.

By the time they got to Reed's turn off on highway 371, it was going on ten o'clock in the evening and he gave her several taps of acknowledgment on his horn and then he was gone into the darkness of the woods on his own road. She returned his message and several miles further she arrived in Birch Lake.

As the familiar homes and businesses took shape she found herself excited about being back at last, even if it had only been a short time. Calling ahead, the first place she stopped at was the kennels for Romeo. He apparently recognized her voice as she came in and immediately set up a big commotion and soon had all the dogs barking and jumping in their cages, creating a hullabaloo of racket. She had bent down to greet him and was knocked back on her heels when he came charging from the back room when the keeper had gone back to get him.

"Whoa, whoa Romeo," she admonished him but he jumped right into her arms and then they both toppled backwards on the floor. He licked and washed her face in excitement and finally she got him calmed down. But when it came time to slip him into the carrier, for the trip home, he put his head down between his paws, seemingly in despair and cried. Shaking her head, Daisy just picked him up and carried him out to her car and set him down in the passenger seat. "Now listen buddy," she spoke sternly, "Just don't move and I'll let you get by this time." And she snapped the seat-belt around his quivering body, and he seemed to sigh and then sat down on his haunches. And, if she would have glanced back over at him, she would have seen a doggie smile on his face.

She had also called Sheriff Jesse and informed him she was on the way back, and he said he would meet her at her house and see that she got in okay. His LTD was parked at her place when she sped into her driveway.

She opened the car door and Romeo jumped out of the seat-belt and was out even before her. Sheriff Jesse helped her gather her things and then she unlocked the door and stepped into her house.

She flicked on lights and stood for a minute just inside the door and looked around. This was the moment she had wondered about. Would she love it again or would she still be afraid to stay in there? Romeo scampered in and immediately put his nose to the floor and ran off.

Sheriff Jesse walked in ahead of her then. "Listen Daisy, do you want me to go around and check things out?"

She smiled at her friend. "Oh God, would you please, Jesse?" She asked then relieved at his offer. And she went to the counter and perched on a stool and looked around the corners of the room suspiciously. She heard him opening and closing doors and drawers, shaking hangers in closets and even moving furniture back and forth. He was busy for a good ten minutes as she sat patiently perched at the kitchen counter.

Finally coming back, puffing somewhat, the sheriff informed her, the house looked safe and free of any crawly marauders.

He carried her suitcases into the bedroom and said goodnight, and she closed the door and called Romeo. It took several times before he apparently heard her and came scrambling out to the kitchen. He had a dust ball stuck to his nose and his mouth was full, and he went directly to his gifting spot and lay his offerings down.

Daisy was almost afraid to look, but when she dared step closer and bend down, she saw something horrible. He had found a perfect casing of snakeskin that had been shed, but no animal inside it.

"Oh God," she whispered and looked around nervously. "Where did you find this?" She asked. as he whined and danced around her feet. "Do you want to show me?" And when she walked with him, he led her to the library where her collection of hard-cover books was arranged on shelves. And he stopped right in front of a bottom shelf of mysteries and whined. Daisy stopped too, and chills tingled up and down her spine. Well, she wasn't about to look behind there.

"Come on," she said to Romeo. "Let's get out of here!" And running into the bedroom for her suitcases again, she grabbed them, locked up her house and left. Then made her way back to the familiar Birch Lake Motel and signed in for an indefinite stay.

Lyn LaCoursiere

-28-

Reed had to admit it felt good to be home in Birch Lake and done with the stress of chasing down another 'gun for hire'. Now, if that was the last assassin to come to their town, they would be fortunate. "But you just never know," he mumbled, "how long and how deep this affront would go on." And his thoughts were still with Murphy in Minneapolis and he wondered how Murphy would deal with the thirty day suspension without pay, he would most likely get for allowing his gun to be "out of his control."

His house had an unusually quiet feeling to it as he unlocked the front door and stepped into the foyer. Right away, he noticed the usual assortment of Lindy's shoes that she left by the door was missing. Then when he hung his jacket in the closet, the empty hangers that had previously held hers dangled noisily.

Oh hell, he thought then as he went to the kitchen. There everything was in order; no dishes in the sink, the chairs pushed in to the table and the sunflower arrangement in place and the counters clean. The living room was tidy and when he walked into the master bathroom he knew right away Lindy was gone when he saw all her bottles and jars were missing. A feeling of loneliness spread through his chest as he looked into the bedroom, and found she wasn't there either. He stood for a few minutes looking at the empty bed, and he remembered he hadn't called her for a few days. Ah hell, maybe not since he'd left last week.

The he turned on a heel and went back out to the living room and collapsed in his recliner. He put the seat back and rested his head, then he saw the note she had perched against some books on the coffee table. Snapping the seat back upright he reached over for it and began to read.

Reed; By now you must have seen I've taken my things. I've been here alone for days and haven't heard a word from you, or even if you are okay. As I've waited I began to realize your work and your life comes before me, and, I can't change that. I need to leave and take charge of my own life. Thanks for everything. Lindy

He read it and then again as he sat in his recliner. Then he got up and went to his liquor cabinet and poured a healthy shot of Crown Royal.

"Goddammit," he exclaimed to the empty house, "didn't she know I was involved in a chase with a killer?" He let that simmer for a while then swore again. Finally, he had to admit he should have called her and let her in on the events. After another shot of liquor he went to bed, alone and pissed.

As he got up the next day and grudgingly had to make his own coffee, as he looked out his windows he saw to his amazement that his trees were beginning to turn colors. He hadn't realized it was that late in the season. The birch had a touch of gold and red against the blaze of their white trunks and the cottonwoods and the maples had also spiced up their look.

Taking his coffee, he went outside to the dock and walked out to its end. The lake was smooth with only a ripple coming in from a boat and a fisherman out in the distance. Reed stood for a minute and listened to the wonderful quiet. No traffic noise even from the highway. Then in the distance he heard the familiar call of the loon from the family that lived on his shore. Yup, this was what he loved.

Later that morning in town, he stopped over at Ed Harrison's. It took several minutes for Ed to get to the door, but then, there he was opening up and leaning on his crutches.

"Hey buddy," Reed exclaimed, "sorry to get you up but I wanted to see how you're doing."

Ed laughed. "I might be slow, but I get around. Come on in and have some coffee."

"Thanks, but really, how are you?" Reed stepped in and closed the door.

"Well, other than being totally bored, I'm getting better. I can get around on these, as you can see."

"Can I help you with anything or get something uptown for you?" Reed asked as he followed Ed to the kitchen.

"No thanks, I have a housekeeper and a driver, so I get out. I'm going down to the office today to check on things." As he talked, he filled a cup of coffee for Reed and handed it over to him.

"I guess you've heard on TV how things went down yesterday down there." Reed said as he took a seat at the oak table and pulled up a red fabric covered chair that brought out red accents around the room.

"That's all I did. Daisy called and brought me up on it too. Did she get back yet from there?" He asked Reed.

"She followed me and got in about ten thirty last night too. She said Jesse was going to meet her at her house and see that she got in okay." Reed drank his coffee, but noticed Ed seemed almost forlorn suddenly.

"No doubt she was totally wiped out." Ed offered.

"I'm sure, after all this." Then Reed asked, "Has your doc given you a timeline for your recovery?" Reed asked then.

"Oh sure, keep on with physical therapy every day, and then go down to canes next week if he sees improvement. There's no room for sitting around feeling sorry for myself." Ed laughed. Today he was clad in a navy blue workout outfit. His tan looked good against his white t-shirt. But Reed noticed a few more gray hairs had sprung out at his hairline in his thick brown hair. And his usually smiling brown eyes held a shadow of sadness.

"Have you had your boat out at all," he asked Ed, wanting to brighten the conversation.

"Nah, I haven't had the urge. Not since that psycho came onboard and started all this."

"Hey, do you want me to come along and we'll take her out and have a beer?" Reed offered. "Before we know it, we'll be up to our ass in snow."

"Hm--, maybe." Ed said as he raised his cup of coffee.

"Buddy, I'm sure you're going nuts, inside like this. Do you read mysteries or novels?"

"Fuck yes. But, I think I've read everything in my library."

Reed grinned. "Well, you're in for a treat. I have the whole collection of mysteries by author John MacDonald and I swear you'll get hooked."

"Okay thanks. I'll look forward to it." Ed smiled again and seemed more his old self.

After a few more minutes of conversation, Reed stood. "How about you coming along over to the café for breakfast, we'll stop in and see Jesse and then run out to my place and get those books."

"Hey, I think I will. I need to get out of here for a while." And Ed got to his feet with the help of his crutches.

"I'll bring my car around to the door," Reed went on to say. And within a few minutes they were on the road to town, although it had taken a bit of effort for Ed to get into the low slung Corvette.

At the Woodsman Café, Ed was greeted by the usual group of retired guys who gathered daily at the counter for their eggs. Otto, the oldest member was there in his usual attire of bib overalls, flannel shirt and necktie. Today his tie had small pictures of Betty Boop on it.

After encouraging greetings from all them, Flo, the other oldest female in town and head waitress came swishing over on her crepe soles and planted a kiss on his cheek.

"As I live and breathe, I never thought this was possible, for you to be up and getting around so soon!" She exclaimed. Of course, she was in her usual snow white uniform and had a red lacy hanky peeking out of a pocket on her shoulder. Her hair was a gleaming bright red also.

"Come on and sit down, you poor thing." She said and went to the nearest table and pulled out a chair. "Now I'll bring coffee and you look at the menus." She hustled off to the kitchen on a mission for more of her best customers.

After a sumptuous breakfast of bacon, eggs and cakes, Reed and Ed stopped in to see Jesse at the sheriff's office next door.

"I heard Murphy might get suspended for thirty days," Jesse said looking up from his desk as they came in.

"Yeah, he is expecting it." Reed watched Ed sit down. "Here, let me take those for you," he said to him reaching for the canes after he finally settled.

"Nah, thanks I'm good." And Ed leaned them alongside his chair.

"How are you getting along buddy?" Jesse asked looking Ed over. "You've lost weight."

"Yeah, I guess, thought I could stand to lose a few." Ed mumbled.

"I'm trying to talk him into going out on the lake today." Reed said then.

"Well, God almighty, if I got an invitation I'd sure as hell go, but I've got to stay here." Jesse volunteered.

"Thanks Reed for the invite." Ed said, then added, "But I've kinda been waiting to hear from Daisy, but I guess she has my cell number, so she can still reach me out there."

Lyn LaCoursiere

-29-

Daisy woke up to Romeo licking her face and when she pushed him away, he jumped down to the floor and scampered to the door.

"Oh Lord, I suppose now you need to go outside," she mumbled and he woofed his answer.

Slipping on a robe, they both squinted in the bright morning sunlight as she opened the motel door, then Romeo ran out and found a tree.

As Daisy stood there it hit home that she was back at the same cheesy motel that she and Roma had stayed in such a short time ago. So many things had happened since then, it made her head spin. The snakes, the deaths, the will and finally now, the realization that she could not, no matter how many times she had her home pest proofed, she still might not ever be able to live there again.

A breeze blew over from the café down the block bringing with it the mouth- watering scents of breakfast bacon, and the wonderful aroma of fresh brewed coffee. A noisy truck rumbled past on the one main street in front of the motel.

She brushed her silvery hair back off her face and took a deep breath. For God's sake, she had to get busy and make a plan. But first this morning she had to go down town to her shop and see how that was going. Hopefully, her friend had kept up her manicuring business for her these last weeks.

She brushed at the sleeve of her leopard print robe as a fat bee settled on it, then watched as it buzzed off in the sunlight. Taking a deep breath, she stood up and made her way back into the motel, with Romeo scrambling at her heels.

As she stood for a minute to sort through her demands for the day, she still felt at loose ends. She realized she hadn't felt this low for many years. Lately, especially for someone who cared deeply for her, to want her, someone who missed her. Over the years, she'd had boyfriends and occasional lovers, and always felt in control of her love life, but now lately it hit her that she had no one. She almost felt like crying too as she looked around at the place she was living in now, and that her beautiful home stood deserted just a few blocks away. She had to take a good hard look at what to do with it. Could she sell it? Or, would it be always standing empty and be thought of as haunted with "killer snakes".

"For God's sake," she mumbled to herself for letting these negative thoughts get her down. She had to get a grip. And, she knew too, these down thoughts were another facet of grieving. Roma, her best friend was gone, wasn't coming back, ever. But she was here and had to move on.

Her cell rang then, and she hurried to locate it amongst her bed covers. When she heard Ed Harrison's voice at the other end, she felt a little better.

"Good morning Daisy Mae," he said.

"Hi Eddy," she smiled and sat down in the bed and covered up, then plumped a pillow behind her head.

"Reed stopped over and he said you'd gotten home right behind him last night."

"Yes, I did and then Jesse came by." Daisy said watching Romeo's efforts trying to get up in the bed with her.

"So, I bet it feels wonderful to be home again." Ed went on, "It's so good that whole affair is wrapped up, isn't it?"

"Hmm-," was all she could muster at the moment.

Sensing something was amiss, he asked curiously. "Daisy, talk to me, what's going on?"

Daisy took in a breath and hesitated to steady her voice before saying anything.

"Eddy," as she had gotten to calling him lately. "I came back here to the motel last night. I can't live in my house anymore."

"Jesus, why?" He asked.

"Can I come over this morning Eddy, I need to see you, I haven't since all this happened to you."

"Of course. I'll look forward to it. Right now I'm at the Woodsman with Reed, but I'll be back home in a few minutes"

"Thanks," Daisy sighed. "I've missed you, old friend. I'll see you in about an hour then. I need to stop by my shop first though." And, she tossed the covers off herself and hurried to the shower. She dried and gelled her blond hair and then applied her makeup.

"Lady, you look better," she said to her reflection. "Now smile," she scolded and forced her face to do just that before leaving the motel.

As she drove through Birch, she noticed the landscape had silently taken on the look of an early fall with gardens bearing late blooming asters, mums and sunflowers. She saw the sweet corn stalks in backyards stood laden with crops. When she opened the window in the car, a wisp of smoke from the burning bogs prevalent to Northern Minnesota tickled her nose.

At Ed's house by the lake, the red brick gleamed in the morning sun against the blazing white trim. The grass in his yard was still emerald green and of course weed-free. Pots of fall flowers on the patio were brilliant in gold, purples, browns and tans.

MOONBEAMS TOO 217

As soon as she turned in to his circular cobblestone drive, she saw him standing out on the front patio waiting for her. He was wearing dark blue sweats and she waved as she stopped and climbed out of the Porsche. She almost cried, when she got closer and saw his handsome face had become gaunt and thin. He leaned on the crutches as he stood in the doorway. The last time she had seen him was when they had been sitting on the couch together weeks ago, when the killer had gotten into his house, when she had run for her life.

"Oh my God," she whispered now as she hurried up to him. She clasped him in an embrace and tears immediately started to stream down her face. "I'm so sorry," she said, "What those people did to you is unbelievable." They stood in each other's arms for minutes as each felt the warmth of their bodies heal some of their pain.

Ed stood back then and raised his head. "Come on in Daisy," he said then, "and let's sit."

"Okay," Daisy said. "Let me help you," and she held the door as he maneuvered himself on his crutches back inside the house.

"Let's go to the kitchen, my housekeeper's got coffee and cinnamon rolls ready." He said then as he hobbled beside her.

Daisy put her purse down on the counter. "Let me help you, Eddy," she said seeing his struggle. She blew out a breath and looked around helplessly for something to say, something to do. She was responsible for this and all because he had been helping her get through all that madness that had gone down.

She pulled out a chair from the table for him, then filled the coffee cups that stood on the counter ready. Ed leaned over and set the crutches against one of the spare chairs after settling, then turned to her.

"Now Daisy, tell me what's going on." Funny, she hadn't noticed before how his voice sort of took on a special whisper when he talked to her.

And she began to talk. "Eddy, I'd been so anxious to get back home and back to some normalcy after this awful hell we've all encountered. But when I stepped into my house last night I still felt spooked by what had happened in there. I did not feel safe! I still felt there might be more snakes hiding somewhere in there yet." All the while she had been talking she had been stirring her coffee after adding cream. "And, I don't believe I can live there, no matter what I do."

Ed shook his head and now as the sunshine lit up the kitchen, Daisy could see the gray, that had crept into his hairline, and that his brown eyes had lost their usual sparkle. "Daisy," he exclaimed, "You would give up your beautiful home?"

"Honestly, I'd hate to, but I don't know what else to do." She said and tasted her coffee.

"But you love it!" Ed raised an open hand. 'Remember how excited you were to get it built?"

She smiled, then said sadly. "I know."

"But where will you go? What will you do?" He asked.

"I don't know." Daisy murmured. And they were both silent then as they sipped their coffee, adrift in their own thoughts.

Lyn LaCoursiere

-30-

Daisy's own thoughts were scrambled as she sat across from Ed in his kitchen in Birch Lake. His invitation for her to "come in and have some coffee" had been welcome when she had stood at his door feeling so blue. Her stalker was dead and things should finally be normal again, but, when she had gotten back home last night after being in Minneapolis the last week, she had found she just could not stay in that house. He said, "Why don't you stay with me for a while and give yourself time to really think about it."

"Oh," she hesitated, "I can't do that Ed, look what associating with me has done to you."

"Daisy, you can't blame yourself for this." Ed waved a hand in the air as he spoke. 'Listen, I'm a grown man and I made the decision to help you. I do not blame you!"

"Well, I blame myself. Have you thought what the townspeople would say about it, if I did move in with you?"

"Ah-crap, who cares if they do talk, but generally, I think they'll go along with whatever we do."

"Yeah? I'm a little worried about their reaction to all this hoopla, and, I need to think of my business and keep my customers wanting to come to my shop."

Ed smiled and shook his head. "You started something when you opened it Daisy, but I think your customers will continue to need their mani-pedi's."

"I hope so." Daisy murmured and ran her hands through her silver blonde hair.

"Think about this though." Ed exclaimed. "I have a big rambling house and the carpenters are about done with remodeling that wing that got messed up, so you could have the new digs."

"Wow."

"Well, I've had nothing to do since I've been housebound like this," Ed grumbled.

Daisy was torn with guilt; maybe she should stay and take care of him, to repay him for all he'd done for her. Romeo had settled under the table by her chair, and now she could feel him licking her ankles. He was getting restless.

"Ed," she said then, "I need to go back to the motel and catch up with my sleep, before I can make any decisions."

"Okay, but you could do that here. I promise I wouldn't disturb you." Ed said pleading his case.

"You're so sweet, but I need to do this. I'm sorry, I don't take your invitation lightly, but I need some time." Daisy bit her bottom lip. She knew he was looking for more from her, but she just wasn't ready to get involved, if at all, she admitted to herself.

Back at the motel, she tossed her clothes in a chair and crawled back into the blessed comfort of the bed. She pulled the sheets up to her chin and closed her eyes. But restful sleep did not come to her, as the memories of the last few months all came crashing back, vivid and shattering details of holding that gun that killed Gunther, and the raw terror that skittered through her body. The terrible ache in her heart when she learned Roma was dead. And then jealously, as she dreamed that a new blonde summer resident in town seemed to have set her sights on Ed.

And finally then, after she had slain all the demons in her dreams, she fell into a sound sleep. However, a subtle noise or an intuitive alarm awakened her just before daybreak. Curious, she jumped out of bed and peeked out a side window which looked out at the street. There she saw a lone figure hurriedly walking away a few doors down. Too far away however, to clearly see who it might be at this time of the night, or early morning.

Later, Daisy left her motel room to go to her shop. She normally took her Porsche even though it was just a few blocks away, but today something niggled at her inner edges and she decided to leave it there and walk instead. Maybe she'd call Jesse, and just run this strange feeling of unrest she felt today, by him. Almost afraid to put the thought into words that someone could still be out there, after her. Yet again. Her skin crawled at the thought.

She called the sheriff after she reached her shop and told him of seeing that stranger hurrying off in the early dawn, in the dark, and asked, "I'm wondering if you could please have someone check over my car, Jesse. Maybe I'm being too paranoid but I just have a feeling that this stranger might have done something to it."

"Of course, but can you describe that person you saw?" He asked.

"He, or she, was a half a block away and it was just getting daylight. It's hard, but I'd say average height and build, in dark clothes."

"Anything else?" Jesse asked.

Daisy pictured the person again in her mind and then added, excitedly, "Yes, yes, he walked funny."

"How?" Jesse exclaimed.

"Well--, like he had a bad foot, like it dragged slightly or something." Daisy checked her daily appointment book as she spoke.

"Did he resemble anyone you know?" Jesse asked.

"No, too far away and not that I can think of, but I have to admit I'm just a little spooked. And then maybe I'm just imagining all this Jesse."

"Here's what I want you to do Daisy, keep an eye out for any strangers. And call me right away if you even think someone looks suspicious." Jesse warned her.

Hanging up, Daisy opened her shop for her first customer of the day. It was Flo, the senior waitress from the Woodsmen Café for her AM appointment.

"Good morning my dear," Flo said sitting down at the table and not taking a breath exclaimed, "I heard they got that crazy woman who has been trying to kill you!"

Daisy wondered not for the first time, how things could spread so fast in such a slow moving small town.

"Yes, they did get her," she said but didn't elaborate.

"I heard she grabbed a cop's gun and shot herself." Flo went on to say, nonplussed by Daisy's short end of the conversation.

"I don't know all the details Flo, I've been pretty upset."

"Oh my dear, I'm so sorry." Flo purred. And they went on to discuss the weather and the coming winter.

And after getting her faux nails rebuilt and polished, she went next door to the beauty shop for her monthly color redo.

Daisy was so busy she didn't have time for even a quick lunch, that first day back. She finally locked up her doors and sat down with relief at five o'clock. She hadn't heard back from Jesse yet, so she called him.

"I just heard back from the garage Daisy, and here's what the guys found," Jesse was talking faster than usual. "Jesus, you can count your lucky stars that you had that feeling this morning and didn't get in your car!"

"Why?" She asked sitting up straighter.

"Jesus," he said again. "Oh sorry," he apologized, "Listen, they found enough juice under it to blow half the town to kingdom come!" He blew out a breath.

"Ohh--," was all she could say, and could feel a chilling wave of fear spread down over her body. "What should I do?" She finally managed to ask.

"Don't be alone, for one thing." And added, "Daisy, go and stay with Ed. He's got more guards there now."

But, she hung up the phone sat in a daze. Now she really was in trouble. Before she'd had her reliable Porsche to get away in, now she had nothing. No car, no home and no friends whom she could run to for safety, nobody that she dared to involve in her trouble again.

She turned off the lights in her shop and sat in the darkness, then leaned her head down on her arms and closed her eyes. For the first time in a long time, she was totally alone.

-31-

Reed loaded his collection of the John MacDonald mysteries in a box for Ed and after sharing a couple of beers out on his dock, it was now getting to be a late afternoon and they were on the road back into Birch.

"Buddy, do you want to take your boat out this evening?" Reed asked Ed.

"Nah, I'm not in the mood. I've been thinking about selling it." Ed sat slumped down in the seat and his knees almost hit the dashboard on his side of the Corvette.

"Why?" Reed asked. "You've always had one."

"Yeah, but I'm tired of it."

"Ed, what the hell is wrong. You live on the water, man." Reed exclaimed to his friend.

Ed was silent, and then took out his cigarettes, rolled the window down and lit up. He smoked in silence for a few minutes as they sped through the wooded area and then approached the outskirts of Birch Lake, and soon went by his place of business and car lot.

"You see all those cars, old and new, hundreds of thousands of bucks?"

"Yeah," Reed answered, puzzled at his friends sudden outburst.

"Well, I've got to take a big loss. There's been paint sprayed and splattered on almost all my outside inventory."

"What the hell! When did this happen?" Reed asked frowning.

"Sometime last night! My service guy called me when he got there about 5:00 this morning to do some work," Ed said, then continued, "I've got a call in to see if and how my insurance stands on this."

"Goddamn, you say paint?" Reed put the Corvette in fourth gear as they roared onto highway 371.

"Yeah, what the hell is this about anyway?" Ed blew a disgusted cloud of smoke out the window.

Just then Reed's cell rang and he heard Jesse say, "Reed, can you come down to my office immediately?"

"Right now?" Reed wanted to know.

"Christ yes, I've got another incident on my hands here, and I might need some help." Jesse was breathing hard.

"I'll be there in five minutes, Jesse. What's going on?" Reed asked.

"Listen, we found a bomb in Daisy's car!" Jesse was talking fast.

"A bomb? Is she okay?" Reed blew out a breath as he listened.

Ed caught the end of the conversation, and sat up and yelled, "You say, now a fucking bomb?" He repeated.

"Yeah, yeah she's okay. That's right!" Jesse answered hearing Ed's remark. "She saw someone lurking around the parking lot over at the motel before sunrise this morning and had enough sense not to get near her car."

"Where is she now?" Ed asked loud enough so Jesse could hear him.

"At her shop. I told her to call you Ed."

"Okay, we'll go by there." Reed clicked off his cell as they got into town. Turning to Ed, he said, "So now we've got someone who is trying to demolish your inventory and then attempting to murder Daisy, again. I can't believe it's all starting one more time."

"For Christ's sake," Ed said in disbelief. "What the hell do we do?"

Reed shook his head. "First off, we better call FBI agent MacGreger back and have him bring in the troops."

"How do these fuckers get their messages back and forth so fast? These gun slingers from over there are unrelenting!" Ed grumbled.

Reed brought the Corvette to a quick stop on the street in front of the building that housed Daisy's manicuring business. Right off, they could see her lights were out.

"Where would she have gone?" Reed asked turning to face Ed.

"Christ, I don't know but we better check the motel." And then added, "I don't think she'd go near her house."

At the motel, they found she hadn't been there, and when they drove by her house, it stood dark and forlorn looking in the early evening.

"Where would she have gone?" Reed asked. "Who else would she have gone to stay with?"

"I don't know man." Ed commented dryly. "But I'm sure she has more friends then I'm aware of."

Next, they parked in the sheriff's lot and climbed out of the Corvette. Inside Jesse's office they found him on the phone, red in the face and apparently stressed to the max. Slamming the phone down minutes later, he exclaimed, "The bastards want me to lock down the town, now. It'll start a panic, and just how the hell can I manage that with one deputy on board."

"The feds, I take it?" Reed asked.

"One and the same, I was trying to locate MacGreger and I got one of them other assholes instead." Jesse stood up and shrugged his shoulders a few times. "Did you pick up Daisy?" He asked then.

"No, we couldn't find her, the shop was dark and she was not yet at the motel." Ed said, sitting down in a chair and leaning the crutches against another.

"I just talked to her." Jesse remarked. "Jesus, she's got to be scared shitless."

Reed and Ed agreed. "Here's what I think," Jesse went on to say, "I think it would be futile to lock down the town. For Christ's sake, this asshole has had all day and I can't believe he or she would still be hanging around close. And, I think they would be listening for news about the bomb, and since there is none, I'd also bet however, they'd be somewhere close by, waiting and watching just over a hill, somewhere."

"What can we do to help, Jesse?" Reed asked.

By now it was going on 7:00 in the evening and the sky was dark and threatening. Streaks of lightening shot over the heavens and the air was heavy with humidity. A small fan stood on Jesse's desk blowing in his face but did little to cool his florid complexion.

"I have to get word to our residents to stay inside." He said then, wiping at his face.

"Right now, I'd venture to guess, they're mostly all over at the Legion," Ed brought up.

Reed suggested, "Jesse, why don't you give Ginny, the bartender a call. That it's a direct order from you. Close up and tell everyone to go home, lock their doors and stay inside." Reed suggested.

"Ask her if Daisy is there, too will you please?" Ed asked anxiously.

That done and after it was reported that Daisy had not been there, Jesse hung up.

And seeing Jesse's hands shake clicking off the phone, Reed asked. "Hey buddy, did you eat dinner?"

"Nah, haven't had time, and I can't leave." He said and his voice went hoarse.

Reed jumped up into action saying, "I'll go over and have Flo pack up some food for you. And Ed, should I take you home?"

"Yeah, thanks, I want to be there in case Daisy calls."

So Reed and Ed left Jesse then to the ringing phones from the alarmed residents of Birch Lake as another confrontation struck this usually peaceful small town. And several hours later, going on nine o'clock it was totally silent.

-32-

Some residents living in Birch Lake complained about having the huge bell chime the time as it echoed each peal of the hour, then one chime again on the half hour. But it had hung in its tower high above the town, for decades, originally purchased by its forefathers who had founded the fertile land and the spring fed lake. It had been polished reverently by its inhabitants over time, and the structure checked for wear. As the booming echoed nine PM in the now subdued town, Daisy lifted her head off her numb arms and looked around in surprise. For God's sake, she'd fallen into an exhausted sleep and now the room was dark, except for a sliver of light at the bottom of the shade, from a streetlight just outside. She got to her feet and peeked out. Then, saw there wasn't a single car out there on the street. Not a single one, not even one by the Legion up the block. Nobody!

What the hell? And then a chilling thought surfaced like something out of a familiar movie. Had everyone left town and she had been left behind, alone? Something told her not to turn on a light.

She sucked in her breath as she stood in the darkened room that housed her business and for the life of her she couldn't fathom where everyone was? There was always someone at the Legion at this time of the night. By now it should be vibrating with the beat of music, which sometimes late like this, could be heard all over town. But the town stood quiet and dark, except for the street lights which cast forlorn shadows against an occasional bush or tree.

Daisy stepped back from the window and went back to her chair in her small shop. She sat quiet, and scared. Then jumping up and going to the window again, she could just barely make out Jesse's office windows in the next block from hers, but thought they looked black as well.

It seemed to her the whole town was dark, but of course it only covered a two block space. She did not know that everyone was at home and locked down as their sheriff had directed.

She put a sweater on over her pink uniform and then remembered that her cell phone was lying on her desk. She picked it up, but saw that it was dead. No wonder she hadn't gotten any calls. She plugged it in, but knew it would be a few minutes before it came to life.

She wondered where Ed was, she hadn't talked to him since the day before. Even if she wanted to involve him in her troubles again, she couldn't. As she sat there in her dark shop, an occasional thump and bang coming from the old building made her start in alarm time and again. As the aged boards and pipes settled down after an influx of action from the busy beauty shop and her nail business that day. After a time, that settled down too and all that remained was an eerie creak of the old metal sign hanging over the well-diggers business in the next block.

She fumbled in her purse for her pack of Marlboros and lit a cigarette, something she never did in her shop. But for God's sake, this was different. No telling how long she would have to stay there.

She worried if her car was ready. And if she walked over to the garage, would it be parked outside ready for her to drive? Or would it still have that bomb attached to it?

Oh, for God's sake, how could this be happening? Hadn't she had enough drama in her life already? She could not help but be angry. After all, it had been Roma who had been the target of that mad-man's endeavors. Not her! Not her friends or her town!

Roma was the one, albeit, who had unknowingly become involved with a "gun for hire" over the seas in Norway. When Roma had found out his chosen employment, she had tried to get away from this killer by coming to the US to make a new life! But they had found and killed her. Apparently this circle of like-minded assassins feared Roma had whispered their identity to her best friend, Daisy O'Dell. And after they had gotten rid of Roma Hurst, now her friend, the blonde haired slut was proving to be a hindrance to their secret club which encompassed the world as she had shot their leader, Gunther Mueller.

As Daisy sat there in silent darkness, she jumped as her cell came to life and beeped. Clutching it, it took a minute before she could think clearly of whom she could safely call.

When Billy Miller answered her call for help in Minneapolis, he did sound surprised to hear from her. Then she went into the reason why she called him.

"Are you telling me you are holed up in your shop without a safe place to go to and you're stranded there because your car has a bomb on it?" He asked in disbelief.

"That's about it, Billy. I'm sorry to call you, but the whole town is dark, it looks like everyone has left!

"That can't be, but Jesus, it sounds like you need to get out of there, and fast."

Daisy huffed out a breath. "I've got nowhere I can go to now. They found me down there, and then again when I came back here."

"Give me a minute Daisy. I've got to make some calls. Stay right there and I'll call you back in a few minutes." And the first call was to his acquaintance and friend, Reed Conners, right there in Birch Lake.

Picking up, Reed heard Billy exclaim, "What the hell is going on there in your berg Conners? Daisy is holed up in her shop thinking the whole town has left her there by herself!"

"Huh, what?" Reed mumbled. He had dropped Ed off at his house and was now waiting for a container of take-out supper for Jesse from the candle-lit Woodsmen Café.

Miller went on to say, "A bomb in her car now? Jesus, she asked me for help because she doesn't want to involve someone there again."

"Yeah?" Reed exclaimed. "Here's an idea, if I meet you half way, can you have her go to that same safe house again? But just until we figure out what the hell to do."

"Listen, here is a better idea," Billy Miller added. "I have a plane. Go to Brainerd and I'll meet you there in two hours."

"Better still." Reed had Jesse's box of supper under his arm and hurried to his darkened office where Jesse also sat waiting with phone in hand near a small burning candle.

Handing the carton of hot food to his famished buddy, Reed said. "I need to go by Daisy's office and rescue her, as she's been holed up there for hours."

"I told her hours ago to get over to Ed's house right away." Jesse exclaimed as he unwrapped a burger.

"Yeah, well," Reed said. "She refused to get him involved again."

"Well, what the hell can we do this time?" Jesse talked around the burger he was hurriedly eating.

"I'm going by there again, to get her and bring her to Brainerd and Miller is going to fly there, pick her up and get her to somewhere safe again." Reed was talking as he made his way to the door. "I'll get back as soon as I can," and was gone.

And now, speeding up to the door of Daisy's building, which was a block away, she stepped out of the darkened place and scrambled into the Corvette.

-33-

"For God's sake, how many times do we have to do this?" Daisy exclaimed as she slipped quickly into Reed's Corvette as he stopped at her building to pick her up. Billy Miller had called her back with the plan. He had said, 'Reed will bring you to the airport in Brainerd and I'll pick you up." After just coming back to Birch Lake yesterday and finding out someone was still trying to get her by putting that bomb in her car, the new revelation had just been too devastating that yet another "gun for hire" was in line to get her. She had run out of ideas.

"I don't know what Mr. Miller has in mind for me. I was at a "safe house" before and that was okay, but I told him I do not want to go there again."

"Why not?" Reed asked her.

"I will go absolutely nuts." Daisy exclaimed. "I'm not a prisoner that needs to be locked up."

"But you have protection there, Daisy." Reed argued.

"Yes, I know. But it's not for me." She was adamant. "I know what I will do, so for your own protection I am not going to tell you anything about it."

"Well, how about Ed?" Reed asked. "You know he's got a thing for you, and he's at home right now waiting to hear from you."

"Ed is a super guy. But I almost got him killed, and I can't let something else happen to him." Daisy's voice took on a note of apprehension as she talked now. "I've been hanging on to my friend's coat sleeves too much lately and I have to quit."

"Goddammit, Daisy, what are you talking about? This is what friends are for!"

Reed huffed.

"Yes and no. Look at what happened to Ed for being my friend." Daisy murmured as she brushed at the blue pants to the outfit she had slipped on at her shop. Always one to plan ahead she had several summer things that she left at her shop for emergencies, and if needed, also extra make-up. And this time it was all needed.

"It was not your fault that lunatic shot up his office, Daisy. Ed will be well again and back to his fun-loving self."

"Hmm-," Daisy murmured again, feeling the whole world was on her shoulders. Well, she couldn't hang around waiting for more lives to be lost or ruined. And she would get on that plane in Brainerd.

The hour long ride to Brainerd was over finally and Daisy climbed out of Reed's car at the hanger that Billy Miller had directed them to. She gave Reed a hug as Miller stood holding the passenger door open for her. After the men had exchanged greetings, in minutes she leaned back in the seat and closed her eyes in relief as they taxied down a runway. Miller was busy piloting the craft into take-off, and then leveled off into the star filled skies minutes later. He motioned for her to slip the earphones on that hung on the back of a seat. Doing this, he said to her, "When we get to Minneapolis, you can stay at my apartment downtown tonight. You'll be safe there."

Daisy swallowed over tears of gratitude and shook her head. "No, Billy, I can't take any more of your time. You've done more than a friend should, so I'm going to disappear when we get there. And, I will reimburse you for this trip."

"Daisy, what are you talking about? You've got a whole crazed country after you by now. They won't quit until they see you on a slab."

Chills spread over her back at that. 'Well, what can I do?" She asked helplessly.

"Just stay alive, my dear. Listen, I know Reed and his buddies have got a plan."

"Yeah? Like what?" Daisy's voice rose above the engine noise.

"It's too soon to talk about. But they will be getting together later to put the plan into action."

This news temporarily silenced Daisy and she settled back in the seat and let the droning engine noise lull her into a daze filled slump. As the lights of Minneapolis began to light up the skies, Miller spoke, "Take a look at this magnificent scene, Daisy, it makes a person realize how small we really are compared to this immense showpiece."

Daisy sat up and looked around in awe. The heavens were lit up like a huge Christmas tree with colored lights and it felt as though they were in the middle of it all.

It was breathtaking and she sat spellbound by the glorious sight, thinking, 'I feel like a small child seeing Christmas for the first time.'

"Check your seatbelt," Miller reminded her as they approached the airport in Minneapolis. "I'll let you out on the tarmac by the entrance door to the hanger/coffee shop, and take a seat just inside. It'll take me a few minutes to put this baby to bed then I'll come inside and we'll take off."

"Hm--," was all Daisy could muster, as she was busy unhooking her belt, then taking her bag and purse, she hastily stepped down to a stool a maintenance man had put down for her. The tarmac was busy as numerous planes were unloading and anxious passengers were darting here and there.

A few minutes before Daisy had boarded Billy Miller's plane, she had been on the phone to a car rental office here and reserved a car. Now she hurried in one door and out the other to pick it up, and after paying cash, inside of ten minutes she was in a white late model Chevrolet speeding out of Minneapolis, heading northwest.

It was about a five hour drive and to ease her nerves, Daisy turned the radio up loud and sang to the latest hits coming out of a station in Nashville. Then as the familiar countryside began to appear, she recalled the times as youngsters she had gone with her cousin, Lindy Lewis, to visit with their numerous aunts and uncles who farmed and lived around the area. Now they were all gone, but the kids had inherited the land and some of them had stayed on to make lives for themselves and start families. A favorite niece and her husband had built a lovely home, a mansion really, on a small piece of land, but soon found their business took them away too often and closed up the place. When Daisy had called to see if she could rent it, the answer was yes, but they would not take any money for it. "The freezer is full of food, so eat it up. Your room is still there and we are just happy to have you finally use it."

"One thing though, can you keep this a secret?" Daisy had asked.

"Well, of course," her niece had said. "But I have to let Dick and Judy know. They live just across the field and keep an eye on the place for us."

"Just them, okay?" Daisy had breathed a sigh of relief after the arrangement was made. And now as she drove up to the house, she got out and found the key to the garage door and drove the car in and closed the door. Then, stepping into the foyer from there she stood for a minute and gazed at the magnificence of the rooms. A stairway like the one in the movie called "*Gone with the Wind*" that Scarlet O'Hara came floating down on, wearing that infamous gown made out of the upstairs drapes, occupied one wall. A baby grand piano took up another, and lovely fabric covered contemporary furniture, tables, lamps and original art work was arranged tastefully around the room. Peeking into the dining area, she saw a huge table that could easily seat ten people. The kitchen was full of stainless steel appliances and granite covered countertops. Looking around Daisy saw the color accent was blazing red, and recognized it as also being her niece's favorite color in her clothes.

Daisy brought her bags in and went up the stairs and found the corner room that her niece had always said, "I've got a room just for you, so come and visit sometime. We call it Daisy's room!"

Now she looked around at the hand crocheted bedspread, the fluffy rugs and lace curtains and a lump came in her throat. For God's sake, here her little niece had made a room for her and she had never come to visit. Never taken the time!

"Oh damn," Daisy murmured as she opened her bag. She hadn't had any of her robes or night clothes at her shop when she had tossed her meager things together, and now she just wanted to take off everything and feel the softness of a robe. Tiptoeing into the huge master bedroom she peeked into the closet and found a furry leopard robe. She put it on, and then went downstairs to put the kettle on for a cup of tea. She would be fine here, at least for a few days. However, then she needed to move on as for the life of her, she couldn't involve her family in this incessant murdering spree.

Lyn LaCoursiere

-34-

After attorney Billy Miller had handed his Air Stream model 54 over to the maintenance crew in the small plane area, he strode into the hanger/coffee shop and looked around for Daisy, expecting to see her huddled in a corner in one of the booths. When he didn't see her there, he thought she must be in the restroom and stood there waiting expectantly for her to come out. When about ten minutes went by and she didn't appear, he just went in there himself to see what the holdup was. And not finding her, he muttered, "what the hell?" Several women were just leaving the place and gave him a dirty look.

Back in the coffee shop, Billy Miller just stood there for a minute. He had her cell phone number in his cell directory, so he called it but it rang and rang without an answer.

"What the hell," he muttered again. "Where the hell did she go?" He took a seat at the small lunch counter across the room and ordered a cup of coffee from the matronly waitress who had been sitting reading a magazine. He had needed to see her too and tell her what was happening with the Roma Hurst case. That it looked good so far as her sons apparently were not going to contest her action.

A good half hour went by and she had not come back in to the coffee shop and Miller was in a quandary. The waitress came by then and offered more coffee and suggested a sandwich.

"I don't think so, but thanks for asking," Miller said. Then he asked her, "By any chance, did you notice a blonde lady wearing a blue outfit come in about forty-five minutes ago?"

The waitress smiled at him. "Well, yes, I did. I thought to myself how pretty she is."

"Well, did it look like she was waiting?" He went on.

"No sir. She sailed in here and out the door to the walkway in seconds."

"Thank you," he said then and stood.

By now, it was going on two AM, and the terminal was still bustling with planes coming and going, and people hurrying in every direction. But he still eyed the crowds just in case she was still there. But after another few minutes he gave up and called Reed as he got to his SUV.

"She what?" Reed exclaimed after Millers first words.

"I told her to wait in the hanger's coffee shop for a few minutes while I closed up the plane, and when I came in a waitress said she came in one door and left by another."

"Oh hell, I was afraid of that." Reed exclaimed. "I should have warned you, she was pretty nervous on the way to Brainerd."

"Now what?" Miller asked.

"Now, all we can do is just wait to see if she contacts us." Reed said. Actually he had just gotten home from the two hour trip to Brainerd. And after checking in with Jesse they had both decided to call it a night and catch a few hours of shut eye. But first he got a beer out of the refrigerator and settled down in his recliner to think about this.

So now, not only was Lindy out there somewhere, Daisy had flown the coop as well.

"What the hell is wrong with these cousins?" He mumbled to the walls. "Apparently the wanderlust gene runs in their family!"

And not finding any answers to this dilemma, he tipped the beer bottle up for the last few drops and mumbled, "God damn it," to the walls on his way to bed. Then stopped dead in his tracks as a new thought hit him square in the face. Instead of mumbling, his throat closed over a lump of fear as he realized, Daisy could have been kidnapped and was right now being silenced for good.

-35-

Daisy sat in her niece's kitchen and slowly drank her cup of tea. Her eyelids drooped over her tired eyes and her back hurt like hell. She knew from sitting tensed up for the last hours; first riding in Reed's Corvette to Brainerd, then the plane ride to Minneapolis, and finally the drive from there to here in northern Minnesota. But how long would it be before the people, who had put the bomb in her Porsche, would find her here?

Now she went up the elegant stairway again to the guestroom, and slid under the covers and inside of five minutes she was asleep and snoring lightly. The clock on the bedside table almost went around again before she awoke, as it was early in the morning again. When she tried to move and get out of bed, she groaned aloud at how stiffness had invaded her body.

The big house stood silent and almost foreboding as she lay in the bed and thought over her actions. Reed and especially Ed would wonder where the hell she had disappeared to. And then her attorney, Billy Miller too! But she would not contact them; she would take care of herself and not involve them any further.

She had awakened with a plan, and a good one! She would go west to the Dakota's vast oil fields, and get lost in the mass of people seeking their fortune. But one of the first things she needed to do was get rid of the rental car she had been driving. She had brought her laptop computer along and had located a late model car for sale through the ads from a private party. So after one night, now she was on her way to Grand Forks, North Dakota to pick it up.

A few hours later, Daisy met the private party that had the 2009 blue Ford Fairlane for sale, with low mileage and good tires. The price was three thousand dollars.

"I've got cash, so will you take two twenty five for it?" Daisy bargained.

The seller had long unkempt hair, spoke with a lisp and looked like an "aged hippy."

"Is your money good? You better not give me hot bills!" He said. They were standing outside his house which had a decrepit look to it, needing paint and new shingles. A woman came and stood inside the screen door and listened.

"The cash is good. But I need a favor."

He nodded his head, "Okay, I'll take the two thousand twenty five bucks, but what's the favor?"

"Listen, I'll give you that but I need your help. I'm driving a rental and I need to return it to the rental place at the airport here in Grand Forks. I'll give you the cash if you'll follow me over there." She could see his eyes light up now.

"Well, let me check with the Missus," and he walked over to the door where she was standing and listening. After a whispered conversation he came back over.

"Well, she says the ride would be nice. But those wheels aren't hot are they?"

"Oh heavens no!" Daisy smiled. "I rented it and then my husband saw your ad and told me to make the arrangements. You see I'm meeting him in California."

"Seems okay to me then. I'll get the papers." Turning back then apparently remembered seeing it on TV, asked, "I'll need to see your ID please." He turned again and went inside and left her standing outside on the porch.

"Christ woman, where are those fucking papers?" She heard him mumble, then exclaim as he apparently found them. Daisy had the bundle of cash ready and could feel their eyes burn in anticipation when they both stepped back outside again to the porch.

"Okay." Daisy said and within minutes, they had dropped off the rental and were down the road in the Ford. Next, she stopped and had the car cleaned and washed throughout to get the stink of weed out of it. Then finally she was off to the west, to get lost in the oil fields of western North Dakota. Now that she was on the road and hopefully far away from any killers, she had time to think.

What should she do with her house back there in Birch Lake? For now, it would be okay with the neighbor taking care of the lawn and Reed looking in, but soon she would have to go back. She still had the arrangement with the owner of the beauty shop back there too; that she could continue to run the manicure business, but only temporarily. She also worried about what was happening with the case Billy Miller was working on for her.

It was getting dark as she neared the town of golden dreams as drilling towers soon dotted the oil fields as far as the eye could see on both sides of the already run down busy highway. Suddenly the road filled up with every kind of vehicle imaginable edging its way into the city. She put her window down and soon music filled the air from the cars as its exhausted field workers made their way back to town to fall into bed and do it all again the next morning. As she got closer to the city, she saw parks and campgrounds line the highway holding every kind of RV and tent she had ever seen, and which seemed to extend for miles. As she edged her way along the crowded road, wolf whistles filled the air from the carloads of men. Then traffic came to a standstill and she saw that she was stuck in a traffic jam that extended as far ahead and as far behind as her eye could see!

Lyn LaCoursiere

-37-

It took a long time before Reed could get to sleep after being hit with the realization that perhaps the reason Daisy had disappeared could have been, because right after getting off the plane in Minneapolis, she had been taken!

"God damn," he swore as he sat on the side of his bed. Was that possible?

Had another of those assholes from across the ocean gotten ahead of them again?

Reed picked up the phone but then put it down again. Who could he call anyway?

Jesse was going nuts over this and Miller had said he'd call if Daisy showed up. Ed had worn out the phone lines trying to find her.

Finally, after smoking a couple of cigarettes and a shot or two of Crown Royal out on his deck, Reed pulled his bed covers up and crashed.

Some short hours later, opening his eyes at the crack of dawn, he jumped out of bed with an idea. Then settling down with his coffee, he carefully thought it out.

It could work! He slapped one fist into his other hand and exclaimed, yes! Then watched the clock until the time was decent enough to call Jesse.

"Jesse," Reed said, "I've got an idea that might work that could end this murdering spree these assholes have in for us."

"Yeah? Beats anything I've been able to come up with yet." Jesse had just gotten out of the shower and stood in a towel with his first cup of coffee. It was five AM on a Friday morning in late autumn. Actually, Birch Lake had been having an unusually long Indian summer, and now the brown leaves on the corn stalks rattled in a warm breeze and hundred of leaves danced over the ground, as more lights began to come on over the town.

"I can be over there in a half hour if that works, Jesse!" Reed exclaimed.

"Hell yes, maybe we can have some peace before the natives start moving."

At six, Jesse had a pot of coffee brewing when Reed came into the sheriff's office. Jesse said, "Let's take a walk?" They went outside and started down the street.

Reed was anxious to share. "Jesse, listen to this and tell me what you think. No one knows where Daisy's Porsche is, right?"

"Hell no, Gordie dismantled the bomb and its standing covered up and locked in the back of his shop."

"Who knows about it?" Reed asked.

"No one, only Gordie!" Jesse answered. "I emphatically told him to keep it quiet."

"Good. You remember we figured that whoever is continuing this killing spree, this time would be watching for something to come out in the news about a car exploding?"

"Yeah," Jesse nodded.

"Here's what I thought might work. Let's stage one!" Reed smiled at his buddy.

"Yeah?" Jesse's worry lined face relaxed a bit. "I'm beginning to see it."

"Okay, what do you think? We could get a junker and set it to burn with some accelerants so it would blow up and the parts would be scattered. We plant it in our paper, maybe bury it in a bigger one."

"Okay, I'm seeing it. I know the fuckers are watching for something to happen."

"Here's the thing though, Jesse to really throw them off for good, we need to hint at finding a body. Of course it would be blown to bits and charred beyond recognition. We would need to say something like no information until further notice."

"Christ, we need a real body?" Jesse scratched his head.

"Nah, a cadaver, or I don't know." Reed looked thoughtful as he drank his coffee. "Let's bring the big guy in. MacGreger would know how to do this."

"Good idea, I'll get him on the wire." Jesse picked up his phone and dialed his private number. When FBI agent MacGreger answered, Jesse said, "Buddy, Conners and I are working on a problem and we need your direction."

"Okay. What's happening up there now?"

"Is your line secure?" Jesse inquired.

"Yup, just had it checked again this AM." MacGreger said dryly.

Jesse wiped a hand over his face.

MacGreger went on, "I'm assuming this involves that same problem. Listen, I can be there in time to have an early lunch."

"Great. We'll be waiting. Thanks Mac." And Jesse hung up. "He'll be here for lunch, but we can't let even one iota of this get out!"

Reed smiled and agreed.

-38-

A bright light blasted through Daisy's eyelids as she sat up, instantly awake.

She saw a man standing outside her car, tapping on her window. He held his badge up for her to see. He had on a brown and tan uniform. This was the first time she had seen anyone in official dress in the North Dakota town, but instantly realized he must be a sheriff. She read his lips and understood he wanted her to roll her window down, which she did, but only a few inches.

"Your license and your car registration please," he said gruffly.

Daisy scrambled to get her wits together. It was early dawn and she had parked in a camp ground sometime after midnight last night, to get a few hours of sleep before she ventured further into the busy metropolis.

Half awake now, she realized she hadn't taken the time to register her ownership of this new vehicle or for that matter, change her insurance to cover this one. It was still covering her Porsche back in Birch Lake.

In shaking hands, she located her billfold in her purse, but also to her dismay found her driver's license was not in the usual plastic sleeve. Quickly flicking through the assorted cards, to her alarm found it wasn't there either.

She opened her window a little further down and turned a troubled face to the man and said, "I'm sorry officer, but I can't seem to find any of my identification."

"I'll give you five minutes to locate it, Miss. Stay in your car." And he walked back to his.

Daisy turned and saw he got in a dark brown vehicle that had a light bar on top and spot lights on the side, and now remembered she had seen the name Hansen on his badge. Relieved to see he was the law and not one of those creeps you hear about that dress like one, she grabbed her purse and turned it upside down on the car seat, mumbling, "now where the hell is my driver's license?" She remembered she had shown it to the seller when she had bought the car, when he wanted to see some ID. She was whispering now, "but I'm sure I put it back in my billfold." She tossed things back in her purse but checked carefully now through her charge cards, business cards and even her cash. She checked her pockets and the floor and even reached as far as she could under the seats.

"The damn thing is gone," she groaned. And just then the sheriff came back and stood just outside her window again. By now the sun was up so he didn't have to shine that ungodly flashlight in her face.

"I trust you found your identification Miss," he said and stood expectantly.

"I have lost it." Daisy said to him. "I used it earlier, and it could have fallen out of my pocket this morning at the gas station."

"Could I see your car registration please?" He asked then.

Daisy felt a chill slide down her back knowing she didn't have that either. What the hell could she say now? She could not get into the real reason she was in this God forsaken part of the world. He'd put her in the loony bin. Maybe, just maybe he would let her go with just a warning. She put a forlorn look on her face and said politely, "I just bought this car yesterday, and I've been on the road ever since and haven't had time to take care of the paper work."

She saw the officer take a breath and draw himself up, and then said, "Miss, please hand me the keys and then step out of the vehicle."

Daisy didn't know if she was going to cry from exhaustion or swear as he opened the car door. She exclaimed, "Officer this is a mistake."

"The key please," he said again reaching out his hand and she had no choice but to hand it to him. Then he repeated, "Miss, step out of the car and follow me to my vehicle please," and he waited for her to get out.

"Officer, I'm not a criminal." Daisy replied tearfully.

"You're in trouble Miss." He took her elbow and led her over to his car. When he closed the door, she saw she was in a cage like seat with no way out. No window or door handles.

The officer got in the front. "Officer Hansen here," she heard him say on his cell. "I'm bringing in a vagrant, a woman, who appears to be driving a stolen car. I need a tow truck too please."

Hearing this, Daisy sat up and rattled the mesh screen that separated them. "Officer, that's not true, you've got to believe me. I bought this car, and I had a receipt. I've not done anything unlawful. I'm a respectable resident from Birch Lake in Minnesota."

"Miss, I go by the book. No license, no car registration? You can tell it to the judge," as he started his car.

"Wait, wait please, I need my medicine, my suitcase is in the trunk," she wailed.

A few minutes later, he put his flashing lights on and they got out in the heavy traffic.

Daisy put her head back on the seat and closed her eyes. For God's sake, she was really in trouble. Coming into the crowded and noisy city last night, she had stopped at a campground and parked alongside a trailer. It was going on one AM and her eyes just wouldn't stay open any longer. She had lain down in the seat and covered up with a jacket and in minutes she was asleep until being awakened by the law.

"Officer," she said through the mesh partition. "I can give you names of my attorneys. I am a respected business woman in Birch Lake, Minnesota."

The officer didn't answer.

"Please, I can call people who can vouch for me." Daisy said again.

"Miss, like I said, you have to talk to the judge."

"Oh for God's sake," Daisy said under her breath. Now she was getting scared. She'd read earlier this was a town of thousands of new residents and thought it would be a good cover to hide out in for a while.

On the way in the city, she sat back and looked around. They were in the downtown area and here the lights and signs advertised food, fun and females. The traffic was end to end, horns blasted and music bellowed out of bars and car radios. Even though it was early morning, she wondered were the people here from the night before or were they just starting to party? She didn't realize the town revolved around the shifts of the oil well workmen. And that the liquor flowed 24/7 for these sex hungry, suddenly rich cowboys.

As they turned off a busy street corner that had blazing signs on all four corners that advertised girls, fun and frolics, five men dressed in dust covered field clothes stopped to let the official car by.

"Hey, don't take her away!" One said and slapped the side of the car as it sped away.

Daisy's skin crawled as she began to feel the hungry sexual tension that was the vibe of this suddenly rich and overly crowded western town. She didn't hear Officer Hansen request assistance to meet them at headquarters to stand by so he could safely get her out of his car and inside the precinct.

"Why are we waiting here?" Daisy finally asked Officer Hansen as they had been sitting in his car in the parking lot at the sheriff's office for at least ten minutes.

"Silence please," was all he would say. She didn't see the same men across the street standing, watching with interest. She didn't know there was definitely a shortage of available women in this town and those that were there were making a killing in prostitution.

Soon after his admonishment, another official tan and brown car came rushing up and within seconds she was whisked into the over worked, under staffed, sheriff's office in Surprise, North Dakota.

-39-

Reed sat with Jesse in the sheriff's office in downtown Birch Lake this morning awaiting the arrival of Agent MacGreger. It was going on noon this autumn day and the town was buzzing with activity. School buses rattled by bringing kids home after their half day of preschool and trucks loaded with fresh grain sped through town on their way to the port in Duluth.

Reed mentioned to Jesse," I've been trying to call Daisy on her cell this morning, but apparently she has it turned off."

"Yeah?" Jesse answered. "Do you think she is still in Minneapolis?"

"God damn, I just don't know." Reed swiped a hand through his hair thoughtfully. "She did say she wasn't going to involve any more friends in her trouble."

"It's a little late now, after all the dead bodies stacked up around here, and almost getting Ed too!"

"Yeah," Reed agreed. Just then FBI Agent MacGreger spun up in a black SUV and they stood up to greet him when he came in the door.

"Hey buddy," Jesse said and they all shook hands.

"You haven't done anything yet that I might disapprove of, have you guys?" Agent Mac asked, raising an eyebrow.

"Nope, we've been waiting for you." Reed answered.

"Let's go down to the lake and take a look at the wildlife in the marsh," Jesse said. All three men left the sheriff's office to talk, leaving Millie to tend to any calls that might come in.

As soon as they found a bench and sat down, they began to make the plan.

"Here's what we've been thinking about doing Mac, and we need you to help fine tune it." Jesse started the conversation and Reed picked it up.

"We suspect whoever put that bomb under Daisy's car is waiting to hear of an explosion. So we're thinking of staging one. What do you think? We get a junker and set it to blow up!" Reed lit a cigarette then, Mac listened intently.

"First of all, why not use the real car?" Mac asked.

"Jesus man, it's an eighty grand beauty!" Reed commented. "We think this will work."

"But now here's the kicker," Jesse added. "We need to have a body that ends up blown to bits, which of course is beyond identifying. We need him or them, to think they've finally gotten Daisy, their mark!"

"Okay, understandable, so far I think it could work," Mac said. "But a body?"

Reed exhaled smoke. "Mac, listen to this, we could ask Doc to let us have a piece from one of his cadavers, or see if he could get at least a part of a human for us to use, but hell man, that would take months, and a league of paper to get it off the ground. So listen to this, we use a little beef. It's going to be blown to bits and totally destroyed in the blast."

Max nodded and got out his pipe. Then asked, "Do you have a good spot to set it up?"

"About a mile from here, at a place we call "Four Corners." Reed said. "It's seldom used county roads and they're narrow and winding."

Jesse went on, "Now, we need it to appear in a paper or two, buried on a back page. But only, that a car exploded and burned up after an accident and the driver could not be identified," Jesse went on. "And I'd like to get this together for tonight. "What do you think, Mac?"

Mac took his pipe out of his mouth and blew a cloud of apple scented smoke and asked, "Can Gordie be trusted?" And after being assured that he could, Mac said, "let's go then. Have him meet us."

Jesse called his buddy who owned the garage in Birch to join them. After finalizing plans, they all scattered to get ready to meet again at 3 AM. Reed took off for Brainerd to get a cut of beef after calling ahead. Gordie hurried back to his garage and got one of the old junkers standing in his yard ready. He also got the dangerous fire accelerant that he had on hand for other purposes ready for transport.

The sky was cloudy with intermittent sunshine all through the day. Reed got back from Brainerd with the wrapped purchase in the trunk of the Corvette and went in to his house. He made a sandwich and laid down for a late afternoon nap. Mac checked into the motel, and Jesse and Gordie went about their usual business.

Finally, at a few minutes before 3 AM, Agent Mac swung by to pick up Reed. Gordie took off quietly towing the junker and they all met at "Four Corners." Jesse arrived alone in the event he had to split the scene.

The old roads were seldom traveled and then mostly used by teenagers to the make-out place in the nearby grove of trees. They all quietly closed the doors on their vehicles, as Reed tossed the beef inside the wreck.

"Okay," Jesse said, "Let's do it. They're saying a storm is moving in."

Gordie quickly saturated the junker with the accelerant and set a timer on a lighter. They ran way back, fast.

And exactly five minutes later a loud boom rattled the night and a ball of fire shot up over the tree tops. Shattered leaves fell on their heads and shoulders. Mac took out his cell as they ran back to the scene and snapped pictures.

"Just in case we would need them," he added thoughtfully.

"See that," Reed exclaimed as heat lightning began lighting up the sky here and there. "We couldn't have timed it any better!"

"We don't want it to rain yet though." Jesse wiped at sweat on his forehead.

"It won't take long to melt the metal," Gordie said, "The juice I used will turn that wreck to one big pile of trash."

The gaseous reek of hot metal, hung heavily in the air and then the stink of burnt flesh hit their nostrils as they neared the scene.

"Jesus Christ," Gordie said and suddenly ducked down in the brush to puke. The other men stood and waited for him as he retched.

"You okay, buddy?" Jesse asked minutes later.

Gordie had erased any and all ID on the junker earlier, and it didn't take very long for the torched vehicle to fall in on itself and melt totally into an unidentifiable lump of scrap.

Several days later, buried in small town papers, a two line item read, "Fire caused by accident, destroys vehicle. Identity of driver impossible, FBI agent declares after investigating the scene with Chief Ortega, Sheriff of Birch Lake, Minnesota. A small town nestled in the northwest."

-40-

Daisy had sat wide eyed in the back of the patrol car as they raced through the newly rich oil-town in North Dakota. She saw the place as an alcohol induced cowboy's dream of twenty four hours of fanny's, frolics and fun.

Normally she was level headed and always had thought of herself as savvy, but today she just felt like a total air-head! Just how the hell had she lost everything and gotten into such a mess? Her driver's license for one thing, and then most importantly, the receipt that she had bought the car from that hippy, hundreds of miles ago. Now she was being taken into custody for vagrancy and a thief. Of all things!

Lyn LaCoursiere

For God's sake, she had never even gotten a speeding ticket after all her driving in Minneapolis or anywhere. Here she had been trying to out run a killer, and in her haste loses her ID and all her important papers and right now was on her way to see a judge. Would anyone believe her in this crazy town?

First of all, she needed to get to a telephone and get help from Sheriff Jesse Ortega, back home in Birch Lake, Minnesota. She was sure all she needed to do was to call him and in minutes it would all be straightened out. But for now, after being hustled in to the local sheriff's department, she had been brought to a room and left. Locked in! She had heard the lock click when they had closed the door on her. They had taken her purse and now she sat with nothing. No cell phone, no money, no nothing, locked in a room that had a bad smell.

Her thoughts ran a mile a minute, and she did not like what she was thinking. What would happen next? It was somewhere around mid-morning, so was she lined up to see a judge now or would they drag this on and keep her locked up all day? Her stomach did a flip when she thought back of reading about what could happen to women traveling alone on the road. Just because this was a sheriff's department and should uphold the law, it did not mean that it would. After all, it was run by men. And men were men, the world over. Oh Lord, she was scaring herself.

She put her head down on her arms and closed her eyes. Maybe she could fall asleep for a few minutes and still the ugly thoughts trying to trick her into panicking. It had been still dark when she'd been so rudely awakened this morning by that sheriff and she was so tired. Exhausted really! The time on the road the last few days had taken its toll and she didn't know how long she could keep it up. She just wanted to get to a safe place in a hotel or motel to just sleep and rest for days and then think about what to do then.

She did fall asleep and awoke when someone slammed a door. Lifting her head up off her numb arms, a deputy stood before her.

"Miss O'Dell, I'm here to inform you that the judge is unavailable to hold court today. And then it's the week-end tomorrow so it'll have to be Monday when he can hear the case."

Daisy looked pissed. "What are you talking about?"

"It means you'll have free room and board here for the week-end."

Sitting up abruptly, she yelled, "Here?"

"Yes, ma'am!"

"But you can't keep me here. I need to call my --." Daisy suddenly felt like crying.

This deputy was young and sweating profusely. "You can make a call as soon as we get word from the chief."

Daisy gawked at him in unbelief, then quickly jumped up and dashed for the door.

But the man was faster and grabbed her arm. His bad breath hit her smack in the face as she suddenly stumbled against him.

"Lady, you can't--," he growled as he steadied himself.

"Watch me," she managed to whisper, then struggled to get her own balance.

He straightened and drew himself up, and then walked out of the room slamming the door. It locked again.

Daisy sat there with her gloomy thoughts. Didn't they have to give her access to a phone? Honest to God, just how could they expect her to sit here in their jail for the week-end. What the hell would she do?

At around noon, another deputy came in carrying a brown paper bag which smelled of grease and a Styrofoam cup which might be coffee, she hoped. And after not eating since early in the day yesterday and starved beyond reason, she ripped it open to reveal a burger and soggy French fries. Nothing had tasted as good to her for ages.

Then she sat and waited. Waited, for someone to do something. They couldn't just leave her in there, could they? Damn, now she needed to use the restroom. Just what did they think a woman should do? She got up and pounded on the door. Then banged louder and when no one responded, she yelled as loud as she could.

"Hello, I need a restroom!" After another five minutes when no one came to her rescue, she really got mad. "What the hell am I supposed to do, use a corner?" She yelled again and added, "Now, or else I will sue your department and everyone in it if you don't let me out now!" That finally got their attention and the same deputy appeared this time with a smirk on his face as he unlocked the door. She ran down a hallway to a restroom and relief. When she peered out a little later, the deputy was standing just outside the door waiting for her.

"I'm here to take you back," he said.

"Not until I've made a telephone call," Daisy said then.

"We just heard from the Chief, so if you follow me, you can make your call."

Daisy was too angry to say thanks and followed him to a room. And finally, picking up the receiver she dialed Sheriff Jesse. He picked up on the first ring.

Lyn LaCoursiere

-41-

The local papers in the small towns up north had reported 'Accident burns vehicle and driver beyond identification. FBI closes case.' Jesse sat at his desk in downtown Birch Lake irritated that things were not moving right along.

Now, where in the hell is Daisy? She needs to know what we've done right now before word gets out to her that she's dead! He grumbled again as he read the late edition. God almighty, it looks like she was kidnapped the minute she stepped off Miller's plane in Minneapolis!

He took a swallow of his coffee. But if she would just contact me, I could bring her up on our strategic plan. This time, he felt like they had come up with the best idea yet to rid themselves of the relentless efforts of those assholes from across the pond. For sure now, the killer would have been watching to see that article they had planted in the paper, and believing their mark had finally been quieted when killed in that road accident, he or she, would turn around and go home. And then finally, they could have peace here in the US.

Jesse grumbled again under his breath. He had just a few months until his retirement and he had to go out with a clean slate. It was bad enough that so many deaths had occurred on his watch, but that could be explained by Daisy's friend Roma's bad luck, of getting involved with this unsavory character while living overseas. He liked to think all his people here in the county were intelligent and would understand the misnomer.

He had tossed and turned for several hours after coming back home at daylight after the fire that morning, then had sworn and finally gotten up and stood in the shower for a long time and let the hot water sluice over his tired body. The wife had still been sound asleep so he savored his alone time. As he had scrubbed with a scented gel, he let his imagination go again to his favorite scene; to high up in the mountains in the west to his hideaway. Here his soul-mate, a beautiful woman met him at the gate of her town and let him in to her village where he was young and happy, and all he had to do here was fish the mountains streams and make love. He had never told anyone about his day-dream, but it had given him hours of titillating enjoyment when alone out on a stakeout, or when he just needed to revive his look on life. But now, the water was cooling and he opened the steam filled shower stall, reached for a huge towel and wrapped it around himself. As he dried off, he saw his middle had erupted into quite a "pot" which he didn't like. Aside from that, in the mirror above the sink, he saw his dark brown hair had taken on a nice sprinkling of gray and emphasized his tanned, craggy face. His brown eyes were still good as he didn't need to use cheaters quite yet.

As he slid into his tan and brown uniform, he wondered what he would really do after retirement. Would he dare leave his spoiled and selfish wife and go off to somewhere he would like, or would he let himself be led to one of those boring southern conglomerations where gray haired old people waited to croak.

Now that time was getting closer, and a tingle of excitement ran up and down his back. However, for now he had to concentrate on things at hand.

The phone rang just then as he sat at his desk in downtown Birch and when he barked his greeting, he was taken aback momentarily when he heard Daisy's tired voice.

"Jesse," she said, "I need your help, I'm in jail."

"What the hell-, where are you?" he asked.

"I'm in Surprise, North Dakota. I lost my ID and other papers and now they say, I'm a vagrant and a thief!"

"God almighty, what happened?" He asked.

"Jesse, I bought a used car on the way here and somehow lost the receipt. Then my driver's license disappeared so they've kept me locked up in a room here for hours."

"Daisy, put the phone down and yell for those fuckers to pick it up." Jesse ordered. To which she did and the same deputy rushed into the small room.

"Here," she cried thrusting the phone at him. "He wants to talk to you."

Then stepping aside and in the course of the conversation, she saw the deputy's face flush beet red, and then pale and even heard Jesse's booming voice carry across the room.

At the end of probably three minutes, he hung up and motioned Daisy to follow him saying, "The chief just came in!"

-42-

As Daisy had stood in the Sheriff Department in Surprise, North Dakota, the deputy had muttered "the chief is in," then tossed the phone on to a table and slammed out of the room after listening to Minnesota's Sheriff Jesse Ortega's threatening message.

Grabbing the receiver before it hit the floor, Daisy exclaimed, "Jesse I'm here!"

"Okay listen, the charges are gone. Now, Daisy, hire a taxi and get the hell away from there."

"Jesse, I need to get my car out of the compound, but I don't have a license to drive it." She protested.

"You can always get that car later. Leave now!" Jesse advised.

But listen, here's what I want to tell you. We think it's safe for you to come back."

"Really? How do you know Jesse?"

"Just trust me."

"Are you telling me all this madness is over?" Daisy was almost in tears as she talked to her friend.

"We're pretty sure. Now call me after you get back into Minnesota, I need to brief you on something."

Daisy was ready to run out of there in relief, but she forced herself to slow down. If she ever got away, be darned if she would ever set foot in North Dakota again.

Everything went off as planned and when she saw the Minnesota state line ahead, she couldn't wait to get to back to Birch Lake. Now as she rode in the taxi, she saw the frost had painted the countryside in the night and today the fields of grain stood slightly askew as the stalks lifted their heads in an effort to stand tall to reach the warmth of the sun. Labor Day had come and gone and soon the harvest moon would hover over the land as birds and bees made their annual flights to warmer climates.

Daisy thought of her lovely house standing bare back there in Birch. It had been months since she had been there anxiously waiting for her friend Roma to arrive from Norway, weeks of loneliness and sadness at the turn of events. However, now she worried if she could ever feel safe in her home there.

And what about Ed? It was horrible what had been done to him when that crazed killer had shot at both his knees.

Tears threatened suddenly as she let her emotions wander. Would he ever forgive her for what had been done to him because of her? Without thinking any further, she dialed his number from memory on her new cell.

When he answered on the first ring, Daisy just sat there for a few seconds. And then, catching her breath, she exclaimed, "Eddie, it's me!"

"Daisy, thank God, listen to me!"

"Okay." She said.

"I can walk and I can drive. And I'm on the way to get you!"

"But I'm on the road right now, and I should be there in about four more hours."

"Daisy," Ed said again, "At the next town, stop and call me. Then wait there for me."

"The next town is Detroit Lakes." Daisy said.

"Okay, find a motel and stay there and call me. I'm out the door."

After all her fears and being so alone, Daisy smiled at his abruptness. Always the independent, this felt good to have someone else tell her what to do. She didn't mind at all.

After that, the drive flew by and in Detroit Lakes she found a new looking motel where rooms were available by the water. She paid the taxi-driver, grabbed her suitcase and found her room had a lovely king size bed with all cotton linens and new pillows.

She called Ed when she got in to give him the room number.

"Eddie, I'm here at last," she said and found herself liking the sound of his voice.

"Okay, I'm an hour out, so relax and I'll take care of things."

"Okay," Daisy repeated. "Like what?" she asked curiously.

"I'll tell you when I get there." She heard him chuckle.

Clicking off her cell, she tossed it on the bed and opened her suitcase. Then stepped into the shower and let the warm water curse over her tired and aching muscles. She shampooed her hair, shaved her legs, and then slathered her body in a heavenly smelling lotion.

Slipping into a pink terry cloth shorts and t-shirt set, she gelled her blond hair, did her make-up and finally sat down to relax. Not too many minutes went by until a knock sounded on her door. She had not seen Ed for weeks and when she threw it open, the most handsome man stood there, she caught her breath at Ed's new svelte look.

He had lost weight and stood slim and tanned in black slacks and a white shirt open at the throat with the cuffs turned up. His brown hair was expensively styled and showed just a trace of silver at the sides.

She grinned. "Well, as the saying goes, ''Have you been working out?'"

Ed laughed. "If you want to call learning to walk again working out!"

And then they stepped into each other's arms and kissed. Then Daisy saw the envelope.

Lyn LaCoursiere

-43-

Daisy had looked at Ed in total surprise as he had stepped through the door at the motel in Detroit Lakes. He stood without the aid of a walker or crutches, and with a huge smile on his face.

"I can't believe this," she exclaimed and stood back. "You're walking by yourself!"

"I am. But where the hell have you been?"

"Eddie, I've been hiding out, and I landed in jail."

"I know, I talked to Jesse. Assholes out there!"

"I have never been so humiliated in my life. I was without a single piece of ID. Stupid!" Then Daisy pulled him into the room and the lock clicked. Then they hugged again and this time their kiss went deeper and lasted longer. When she felt his body begin to tremble, she pulled him over to a couch.

"Here, sit down and give your legs a rest." She exclaimed.

"What the hell made you go to North Dakota, Daisy?"

Daisy just shook her head. "You know, I just kept driving in that direction and as I got closer to the MN/ND border, I remembered reading about the huge influx of people going out there." She shook her head then. "But what a bad idea that was!"

"And you bought a car?"

"Well, I couldn't keep driving that rental." Daisy looked worried then. "I bought this car from some people along the way. I paid the guy there extra cash to drive the rental over to the business office in Grand Forks. Good Lord, I can only hope he did."

Ed was silent a minute. "Let me call Jesse and ask him if he will contact the rental company and see what he can find out." He didn't want to scare her and remind her that her name was on the papers. But then she no doubt already knew that.

"I'd appreciate it." Daisy said and her voice took on a nervous hitch as he took out his cell. She began to pace around the room.

The motel in Detroit Lakes was a newly built place in the Grand Hotel chain that Daisy remembered her cousin, Lindy Lewis, had worked for many years in the past when she first started her career. If she remembered clearly, Lindy had met her husband along the way, and had given up her work then to slave over that old mansion they had bought and renovated. The motel here in this resort town was new and lovely and badly needed in this community of summer homes around the lakes. When you checked into one of Grand's "West Wind" enterprises, your needs were all inclusive. The minute they parked your vehicle, you were treated to an experience you wouldn't soon forget.

This particular complex was done with a contemporary theme consisting of gleaming wood floors, rich fabric covered furniture, modern art, and varied colors of blue.

Daisy had been sitting calmly watching Ed and letting her eyes roam around the lovely room, then when she saw him click off his cell, she turned her attention back to him as he said, "Daisy, bad news. This stranger you left that rental car with, never did return it. It's still out on lease in your name!"

Daisy's hopes fell. She had realized later she should not have done something so stupid and left that damnable car with a total stranger, but at the time she was just thinking of getting away from this asshole that was after her again.

"For God's sake, what can I do?" She asked him.

"You've got to report it stolen. What was the name of the town where you bought the new car and left the rental?"

Daisy still paced. She ran a hand through her short hair and remarked, "Someone horse town here just inside the MN border."

"Do you remember the seller's name?" Ed asked.

She closed her eyes and stopped her pacing. "No, but I sure remember where he lives in that town. Normally, I don't let things like this happen Ed, and in my defense, I can only plead temporary insanity.

"Don't worry, here's what we'll do. First, give me the license plate number of the car you bought. The MN attorney general is a friend of mine, so give me thirty minutes." He got back on his cell and began to punch in numbers.

Still feeling terribly irresponsible, Daisy could only mouth the words "thank you."

And after some time, he clicked off his cell and smiled. "Okay, I want you to relax, he's on it. I'll order up a bottle of wine and then we can catch up. Then let's have dinner downstairs in that fine dining room." And soon room service was at the door with a bottle of Cristal champagne and crystal goblets.

The first bubbles that touched Daisy's lips tasted lovely, as she made herself sit down and put her feet up on an ottoman as he joined her.

Again Daisy felt the warm relief of being taken care off. And soon found herself smiling at Ed's humorous tales of his learning to walk again with crutches and canes.

"I'm finding I kind of like not working as much too," He confided. They sat comfortably on the couch and now he put his arm over her shoulder and pulled her into a kiss again. It was tender and she found herself responding and in this kiss, a new feeling spread through their hearts. And they sat back and smiled.

Lyn LaCoursiere

-44-

Daisy sat up in bed and looked at Ed who was sleeping soundly on the next pillow. She tossed the covers aside and smiled, happy as a loon as she made her way to the bathroom. Glancing in the mirror over the sink, she saw even her skin seemed to glow and the tired lines that had so rudely reminded her earlier that time was rushing on, seemed to have diminished.

She took a few minutes to rinse off and then hurried back to the bed where Ed groaned and tucked her back into his arms.

"Now this is heaven," she whispered under her breath and then she too, slept for the first time in days.

The next day, she happily joined him in his SUV and they got on the road back to Birch Lake.

Daisy remarked then, "I wish I felt sure my home was infestation free."

"Listen, I had another company come in, and every single little slip of a hole has been studied and covered. Daisy, they guarantee even ants won't find a place to get in."

"Hmm--," was all she could muster. She realized he had spent a considerable amount of time helping her, so she added, "Thank you, Eddie, I'm just skittish about it yet."

"Well, that's understandable. Just see how it feels for you. And remember, you can always come and live with me." He winked and smiled at her.

The ride through the countryside was colorful as the grain fields had turned golden and harvesting was going full steam ahead with combines busy, and trucks loaded with wheat and flax roared down the highways.

"Tell me Eddie, how are you really feeling now?" Daisy asked as they cruised along smoothly on the freeway.

He turned to her and smiled. "I'm feeling good, especially being with you again."

"Oh yeah?" Daisy joked, and then turned to him. "But I'm still worried though, what if another assassin finds you?"

Ed reached a hand over and patted her knee, saying, "Relax. This time, I'm armed. I'll shoot the fucker even before he or she has time to point their shooter."

"Great Eddie, but I won't relax until I know they've really given up."

"Okay, here's something I think you'll like hearing Daisy. I talked to Jesse before you got up this morning and he's been trying to reach you and bring you up to date. He had some great news for you! Listen to this, a couple of nights ago, Jesse and Reed and this FBI guy arranged a fire and they think these assholes got the message. It's kind of creepy, but here's what they did. First, let me say your Porsche is safely stowed away. So they used a wreck and set it on a hell of a fire out on a country road. After finding that bomb in your car, Jesse and Reed knew the assassin was waiting to hear of an explosion in the newspapers. So they planted one and also added that the driver's remains were beyond identification.

Daisy's face paled as she listened and then sucked in her breath. "You mean, I'm dead?"

"Yes, to the assassins." Ed remarked.

"So what you're saying is that all my friends are thinking I burned up in that fire?" Daisy asked incredulously.

"This is what I wasn't too happy about. But Jesse assured me he'd talked to your family, and he'll explain soon to the people of Birch Lake."

She paused and thought about that. "And they described the car?" She asked.

"Yes, they said it was a late model Porsche." Ed looked over at her. "But no name was mentioned."

"So, now when I go back to live in my house, are my neighbors going to think my ghost is living there?" She exclaimed and it was so farfetched, they both had to laugh.

"Listen," he went on then, "Jesse, Reed and MacGreger made me promise. You're supposed to come to my house for a few days. Their thinking is, the assassin will have seen the item they planted in the paper and finally give up, thinking their work is done."

Daisy just sat, trying to absorb all this drama. The deaths, the snakes, her running and now, finally her own death!

Ed looked at her anxiously. "I'm sorry, are you alright?" After a second glance as he drove, he groaned and shook his head. "Jesus, I told them you'd be upset."

"Eddie," she said at last. "I'm okay. It's just, how am I supposed to react to my own death?"

They arrived back in Birch Lake safely and several nights later, Daisy went over to her house to check on things. But as she breathed in what should have been a familiar scent a homeowner recognizes stepping into their own abode, it seemed to have a lingering sense of violation to it as she stood just inside the door. Even though in the last several days, Ed had hired cleaning people to go over every inch of the place; drawers, closets and every corner. But her personal things had been touched, her privacy invaded, seemingly leaving an offending odor.

She climbed on a stool at the center island and hastily put her feet up off the floor on a rung. Then, gazed around the once familiar kitchen with its gleaming stainless steel appliances, chestnut colored oak cupboards, and red accents that she had so lovingly decorated.

Ed had wanted to come over with her, but she had protested saying she would just stay a minute. She wouldn't turn on any lights.

But he anxiously called her on her cell, and whispered, "Daisy, are you okay?"

"Eddie, I'm fine. Listen, I've made a decision. But I'll tell you shortly." Then she called Billy Miller. The attorney who was handling the case involving Roma's will. The same man whom she'd had a delightful tryst with some weeks ago.

"Well, good to hear your voice, even though you're still dead aren't you?" he asked.

"Yes, for a while yet," Daisy remarked, "Billy, I'm calling to let you know where you'll able to reach me at, as I've decided to sell my house."

"Okay, but you love your home, Daisy. I've heard it's a showplace with the pool and beautiful landscaping."

"Yes, I mean I do, I did." Daisy said slowly. "But I'm sitting here now and I'm having a hard time fighting down the heebie-jeebies."

"Do you still feel there are more snakes in there, Daisy?" He asked.

"I'm thinking I don't want to sleep here," She admitted slowly.

"Well, grab your things and get out, Daisy. Right now, it's looking like your case is going to come through without any problems, and you will soon be a very, very wealthy woman!"

That done, on her next call she said, "Eddie, I'm leaving here now and if that offer still stands for me and Romeo to come back to your house to stay, we're on our way!"

"Al right!" He said excitedly. "And now, you can open that envelope I gave you. I think you'll like my surprise, Daisy. It has our itinerary and we're going to fly out tonight and travel. We are going to see the world!"

***

Later, Sheriff Jesse Ortega called a meeting with the residents of Birch Lake and explained the needed concealment involving Daisy's alleged demise.

The End

Made in the USA
Monee, IL
28 April 2026